The
Homecoming
and Other Stories

Indrani Baruah was born and brought up in the small oil town of Digboi in Assam. After finishing her schooling from Carmel Digboi, she went on to top her batch in English Literature from Dibrugarh University. She has completed her Masters from Gauhati University and is currently an Indian Police Service officer posted in Assam. She is married to her batchmate in service, Parthasarathi Mahanta, and is a mother of two lovely children and a golden Labrador. Her interests include reading, gardening and designing.

She can be reached at indranipmahanta@gmail.com

The
Homecoming
and Other Stories

INDRANI BARUAH

Published by
Rupa Publications India Pvt. Ltd 2023
7/16, Ansari Road, Daryaganj
New Delhi 110002

Sales centres:
Allahabad Bengaluru Chennai
Hyderabad Jaipur Kathmandu
Kolkata Mumbai

Copyright © Indrani Baruah 2023

This is a work of fiction. Names, characters, places and
incidents are either the product of the author's imagination or are
used fictitiously and any resemblance to any actual person, living or dead,
events or locales is entirely coincidental.

All rights reserved.
No part of this publication may be reproduced, transmitted,
or stored in a retrieval system, in any form or by any means,
electronic, mechanical, photocopying, recording or otherwise,
without the prior permission of the publisher.

P-ISBN: 978-93-5702-032-9
E-ISBN: 978-93-5702-036-7

First impression 2023

10 9 8 7 6 5 4 3 2 1

The moral right of the author has been asserted.

Printed in India

This book is sold subject to the condition that it shall not,
by way of trade or otherwise, be lent, resold, hired out, or otherwise
circulated, without the publisher's prior consent, in any form of
binding or cover other than that in which it is published.

To
my parents
the late Dr Harendranath Baruah and
Mrs Nonee Baruah

Contents

An Achiever	1
Ambition	10
Belief	18
The Decision	28
Deity	33
Divine Justice	38
Hope	44
Learning	50
Precious Moments	56
Reflection	62
Religion	69
Remorse	77
Retribution	83
Sacrifice	94
Second Chance	99

The Betrayal	107
The Change	113
The Homecoming	120
The Lost Child	128
The Offer	135
The Prophecy	141
The Trip	151
The Winner	156
Trust	170
Value	176
Vengeance	184
War	192
Acknowledgements	197

An Achiever

Tora had just moved into her parental home. Luckily for her, the house was empty. She had not rented it out. It was Diwali, but for her, there were no lights. It was as if all the lights in her life had been switched off. There was only darkness ahead. Feelings of frustration and hopelessness returned. She tried to quell her fears. She had never dreamt that she would be in such a situation. How had she been so blind? Who was to blame? Her parents, her husband, her family, society, or her fate? Or was she solely responsible for everything? She tried to think and be rational about her position.

But she was tired, tired of her thoughts and her predicament. It was certainly not an easy position to be in, but problems are a part of life. What matters most is how one deals with those problems.

Her wounds would take time to heal. Maybe they would take a lifetime. But she would not break. Not now, or ever. She would fight back. Yes, that is what she will do. She was not the kind of person who would wallow in self-pity. She was on the wrong side of forty.

She had had to face a lot of disadvantages, that was for sure. She would have to strive harder now, but she had never been afraid of hard work. There was only one difference this time. She would work for herself. She would make it work.

With these troubled thoughts, Tora fell into a disturbed slumber.

The early morning rays woke Tora. She was an early riser. For a minute, she stared blankly at her surroundings. Where was she? Then it all came back to her. A feeling of hopelessness and lethargy engulfed her. She had no work to do or anyone to rise for. But old habits die hard. She rose slowly and brushed her teeth. She opened the door and windows, and made some tea for herself.

The memories of the past few days came flooding back to her. Had her life been a lie all these years? She could still not believe the turn of events. She had been married for the past twenty-four years. She had a twenty-two-year-old daughter and a twenty-year-old son. A loving husband.

Tora had been just twenty-two years old when she had married Vikram. He was five years older than her, had a good job and belonged to a respectable family. What more could a girl want? Theirs was an arranged marriage. But Tora had nothing to complain about. Vikram was very clear from the beginning; he did not want his wife to work. His job required him to travel a lot and he wanted a wife who would look after his ageing parents and children.

Tora's parents convinced her. She had already graduated, and since she would not be working, there was no need for her to acquire any other degree. Tora was an average student and she did not mind quitting her studies.

She was a happy-go-lucky girl and she fit into the role her husband had planned for her. She had a younger brother. She looked after her in-laws, gave birth to two beautiful children, and got her sister-in-law married. Her world was perfect. Or so she believed. At least until a week ago.

Actually, her perfect world had started to crumble three months ago. Her parents and brother had passed away in a car crash on their way home from a vacation. Tora was shocked and could not believe that they were no more. It took her a couple of months to get over the tragedy. She performed the last rites mechanically but she could not cry, for her grief was too deep. Her uncles and aunts helped her during this period to perform her duties and she was grateful to them for it. Her father had two younger brothers and their homes were adjacent to her parental home. She got all the support that she needed from both homes.

Vikram was, as usual, away on work. Tora craved his presence. But it was in vain.

She did not make an issue about it. It was not her nature to do so. She quietly went about her work.

Then came the big blow. That was a couple of weeks ago. Vikram wanted a divorce. It came as a bolt from the blue for her.

'But why?' she asked him, bewildered.

'Because I have met someone else. Actually, she has been around for quite some time,' Vikram stated.

She could not believe it. It seemed like a very bad dream.

'But why now?' she questioned.

'I have been meaning to tell you for some time now. I did not want to disturb the children,' Vikram said.

Tora understood. Now that the children had grown up

and left home it would not make much difference to them. Her in-laws had also passed away. She felt used.

For the first few days, she was in denial. She was numb and her mind was blank. But slowly, everything sunk in. Her marriage had been a sham and she had not realized it. She thought of all the times that Vikram had stayed away from home. She had handled all the family problems. He had never shared the burden. She had thought he was too busy professionally to be burdened with other things. She had always tried to make his life easy and smooth.

What a fool she had been. Still was.

She panicked. What would she do now? Where would she go? There was no one to turn to. Her parents and her only brother had passed away. She felt lonely. She did not even have any friends to turn to. Her friends were Vikram's friends. Her school and college friends were long forgotten. She had not maintained ties with them. She had no earnings and was not trained for any job. She could not even afford a good lawyer. What was she to do?

She wanted to wake up from this nightmare. She wished Vikram would tell her that it was all a joke. She was desperate. Her life seemed to be worthless. She prayed but nothing changed.

Slowly, Tora came to terms with reality. Vikram had meant what he said. He wanted a divorce. She decided to sit down and talk it out with him rationally.

Her priority was her children. She asked Vikram about his intentions. Vikram planned on supporting both his children financially as both of them were still studying. Tora was relieved to hear that. He also planned on giving her twenty thousand rupees a month. It was meagre and Tora protested, but Vikram would not budge from his stand. He told her bluntly that he expected her to go back to her parental home and he gave her a month's time to leave their home.

He had planned everything.

Tora was hurt and angry. But she knew she could not do anything. She was being thrown out of the house, like a thing that had long served its purpose. She could do nothing about it.

She went to her parental home, which was located on the outskirts of the city, cleaned and stocked it with food. She decided that she would only take her clothes and move out of Vikram's house. She did not want to take anything else with her. The home that she had built had lost its charm. She broke the news of her separation to her two children over the phone. They were shocked and angry in the beginning, but Tora managed to soothe and allay their fears. She would live in the same city after all. It was just a change of address. She did not wait for the month to end, but decided that the sooner she started life anew, the better for her.

So, by the end of two weeks, Tora shifted to her now empty parental home. It was a good thing that her parents had not remained alive to see this day, she thought. They would have taken it very badly.

The house was a double-storied one. The floor upstairs consisted of three bedrooms and the ground floor consisted of a living room, a dining room and a kitchen. Tora shifted into her old bedroom.

It felt strange to have moved back to her old house after twenty-four years. The house had always been filled with friends, guests and relatives earlier. Her mother was welcoming and popular in the neighbourhood and it felt strange to come back to a quiet house, filled with silence.

With the amount of money that she would receive from Vikram, she could not afford to hire a domestic help. The house was not very large and she knew that she would be able to look after it single-handedly. The garden in front of the house was overgrown due to lack of care. She decided to hire some help and clean it. She would maintain a garden as she loved greenery and nature.

She sipped her coffee as she was consumed by these thoughts. Doing the household chores and cooking would at least keep her busy, she thought wryly.

And so, Tora set about settling into a new routine. Her uncle, aunt and cousins would drop in frequently to check on her and she had a bit of company. At other times, she would sit in the balcony and look around. This had become a favourite place for her. However, a new college had been built adjacent to the house, and she saw the young students of that college and thought of her own kids.

How time flew! Her children called her frequently. That was her only solace.

One morning, Tora was tending to the flowers in her garden when a girl greeted her on her way to college.

'Good morning, aunty,' said the girl.

'Good morning,' replied Tora with a smile.

'You have a beautiful garden, aunty,' complimented the girl. 'I enjoy looking at the beautiful flowers.'

'Thank you,' Tora said, smiling in pleasure. 'What is your name?'

'Jiya, aunty. I am doing my graduation in this college,' she answered. 'See you, aunty. I have a class,' and she waved at Tora.

Tora waved back.

And so this was how Tora started speaking to Jiya and her friends. After a couple of months, she came to know that the college did not have a good canteen. The students did not have any place nearby where they could go to eat and chat, as the college was on the outskirts of the city.

An idea came to Tora. What if she transformed the ground floor of her house into a small restaurant? She was a good cook and could start small. That night, sleep eluded Tora. She was thrilled.

The next morning, she waited eagerly for Jiya and her friends. She asked them what they thought of the idea. The girls were enthusiastic about it. They thought the restaurant would do well. New educational institutions were being set up nearby and so Tora thought and thought. The idea excited and frightened her. She had nothing to lose. Why shouldn't she try?

She asked her cousin. He had started his own business a couple of years ago. He encouraged and promised to help her. Tora now had something to look forward to. She planned and thought out the menu. She wanted to appeal to the younger generation.

Her cousin helped her procure a loan. It took Tora a month and a half to set up the restaurant. She hired a cook and a waiter and then she named her restaurant 'Rendezvous'.

Tora was a good cook. She baked cakes and other snacks. Her prices were reasonable, and very soon, many students learnt about the new place. Her restaurant started to fill up. As the crowds grew, Tora realized that she had to change her menu to cater to other demands.

She was smart and could foresee that her business was

taking off. She hired more help and changed the menu to suit her customers. Soon, her restaurant was a big success and Tora was happy and relieved. The place kept her busy and kept negative thoughts of her marriage and separation away.

Tora was able to pay off her loan in a short time and she soon realized that she had business skills. Her homemaking years had given her adequate experience.

Tora's children visited her during their holidays. They were amazed to see the transformation in their mother. She had become a confident business woman. The students adored her. Her business had grown. She had had to hire help and she even kept it open at night. Even people from the city came over for dinner. Very soon, her cousin proposed for her to open another restaurant in partnership with him in the heart of the city. This time, Tora did not hesitate. She knew she could make it a success.

Tora was making a profit now. It had been a year and a half since she had been asked to leave Vikram's house. He had sent her twenty thousand rupees every month, just as he had promised.

Tora counted the money he had sent over this time and returned it to him. She did not want his money. She did not have to depend on him.

Vikram was surprised when he got the cheque from Tora. He could not understand why Tora had returned the money. He had thought he was being generous.

Vikram had gotten his freedom, but it had come at a cost. His children had become distant from him and his new relationship was not smooth. He had taken Tora for granted. She had always strived to make life smooth for him. He realized that his illicit relationship had been a grave mistake, but he could do nothing about it now.

The next morning, Vikram found his answer in the morning newspaper. Tora's name was all over the front page. She had received an award for being the 'Entrepreneur of the Year' from a well-known organization.

Vikram could not believe it. Tora was an achiever!

Ambition

Shweta and Rohit were an ideal couple. Smart, good-looking and professionally successful. They were also blessed with two beautiful children—a son and a daughter. They were a source of envy within their circle of friends to whom it seemed that god had gifted the two with everything that one could wish for. What more could anyone ask for?

Shweta and Rohit were both officers serving in the Indian Administrative Service. They had been batchmates in the service and had met each other while training. They had hit it off almost immediately. They were attracted to each other, and upon completion of their training, they decided to get married. Their families did not have any objection to the match and their plans to be together went off without a hitch.

Shweta and Rohit were initially posted in separate districts, but they were very practical about it. They worked hard, learning along the way, knowing that the experience would help them in their careers later on. Their time together was precious as it was short. They knew that eventually, they would have time together, after the initial years.

They were first blessed with a son, and then a daughter came along after a couple of years. The children lived with Shweta and were looked after by doting grandparents. After a few years, Shweta and Rohit were posted in the state capital. They had been promoted and held responsible positions by then. Since the children were old enough to go to school, the grandparents went back to their ancestral home, returning for occasional visits.

So it was just the four of them. Shweta and Rohit were busy with their careers and the children were busy with school. The parents took turns to look after the children and the family was a happy one.

But slowly, as they rose higher in rank, their responsibilities grew. They remained in office beyond their scheduled time dealing with many issues, political pressures and competition for good postings from their cadre. And, of course, there were training courses and tours. Twenty-four hours seemed too little, and they started spending less time with the children.

II

Their son did them proud in his tenth standard board examinations by passing out with flying colours.

'What else would you expect?' questioned a colleague. 'The brilliant son of brilliant parents.'

The parents' hearts were swollen with pride. They had never expected anything less. The apparent envy of their colleagues made them feel even better.

Their son, Rahul, had excelled in all subjects. He wanted to study humanities, but his parents would hear none of it. They wanted him to study the sciences and qualify for the

Indian Institute of Technology (IIT). They were confident in his ability to crack it. They had big plans for their son. They refused to hear Rahul's point of view.

Reluctantly, Rahul agreed to their demands.

Their daughter, Juhi, was a couple of years younger than their son. She, too, was doing well academically. She also excelled in extra-curricular activities like debates and quiz competitions and had even represented her school at the state- and all-India level school competitions. Shweta and Rahul were proud of her achievements.

Soon, Rahul was enrolled in a coaching institute to prepare for his IIT entrance examinations. His days were only occupied by academics. School in the morning, followed by coaching classes, and then home to study again. He could not indulge in his favourite pastime—playing tennis. He simply had no time or energy as he was trying his best to cope with his studies.

Meanwhile, Shweta and Rohit were busy with their careers. They were away on frequent tours and also went abroad for work. They barely had time for Rahul and Juhi. But they did not worry about it as the children did not complain.

Soon enough, Rahul wrote his final exams for the eleventh standard and Juhi too wrote her finals for the ninth standard while both the parents were away on a tour. When the results were announced, all hell broke loose. Rahul had done very poorly. He had not even received a passing score in Mathematics and Physics. This came as a big shock to his parents; it was totally unimaginable. Juhi, too, had scored average marks.

Shweta and Rohit wondered as to what had gone wrong with their children, and they came to the same conclusion—that Rahul and Juhi had not studied.

The children were warned and tutors were hired to teach them. Rahul was now more burdened than ever. The parents did not question the children about their poor results. They did not have time to listen.

The atmosphere in the house had grown tense and it no longer had the usual happy and easy air. Shweta and Rohit continued to focus on their careers and social commitments. They did not meet their children's tutors as they did not want to listen to criticism. Unlike other parents, they were used to compliments when it came to their children. This time, however, Shweta resolved that she would take a leave during the upcoming exams to ensure that the children studied.

The next year was going to be crucial. The children were to appear for their twelfth and tenth board examinations. Meanwhile, there was a change in the government of their state. Competition amongst their batchmates for good postings to enhance their positions of power became intense. Rohit and Shweta, too, decided to join the competition. They would not be left behind. They too wanted to hold positions of power in various departments. They worked longer hours to prove their capabilities and came home late. Weekends were spent de-stressing and partying with their friends. They were barely at the house.

From time to time, the children were told that they would have to do well to maintain the prestige of their parents.

The parents did not realize that they were pressurizing the children. Rahul had become withdrawn and was starting to lose weight. Juhi was beginning to get frequent headaches every other morning. But the parents did not notice anything amiss as they were hardly present at home.

The examinations had begun and would last for a month.

Shweta had taken a leave from her office to be with her children. She would drop the children off at the examination centre and pick them up later. During the second week, Shweta went to pick Juhi up from the examination centre. She reached on time and saw the other children streaming out of the centre. Shweta waited for Juhi patiently, sitting inside her vehicle. After sometime, she noticed that the place was nearly empty. But there was no sign of Juhi.

Shweta got down from the vehicle and looked around, but to no avail. Then she ventured into the school premises. She met with some invigilators, but no one could help her.

She started to panic and called Rohit.

Rohit was in the middle of an important meeting and was irritated by the disturbance. But when he heard Shweta panicking, he cut short his meeting and rushed to the examination centre. They started to search for their daughter. All sorts of thoughts crossed their minds. Had she been kidnapped? Where could she be?

They simply had no option so, after a couple of hours, they decided to inform the police. Senior police officers arrived and started investigating. The parents were questioned: 'Who are her friends? Whom was she last seen with? Who is she close to?' The parents did not have any idea. They were usually so far removed from their daughter's life that they really did not have a clue. They were embarrassed by the questions and called Rahul. Rahul appeared scared and answered in monosyllables.

The officers were exasperated. The parents did not have any idea about their daughter's friends and the son seemed reluctant to reveal anything. They were at their wits' end. Meanwhile, Juhi's photos were widely circulated in the media and the police network.

Rohit started to blame Shweta. 'You should know who her friends are,' he said accusingly.

Shweta accused him back. 'You do not know anything about her or Rahul's friends either,' she said defensively.

'But you are the mother!' he stated.

They glared at each other. Then they asked Rahul whether he knew anything. He shook his head silently.

'Why won't you speak to us?' Shweta said in desperation.

'When have you had time for us, Mamma?' Rahul said quietly.

'What do you mean?' Shweta responded in a quivering voice.

'I have dropped out,' replied Rahul in a small voice.

'Dropped out?' questioned Rohit.

'I have not answered my maths paper,' replied Rahul.

'But why?' Shweta was perplexed.

'I will not answer my physics paper either,' replied Rahul defiantly.

'But why?' Rohit and Shweta were bewildered.

'Because I will fail both the papers,' Rahul replied sullenly.

'Why didn't you study?' Rohit grew angry.

'It does not matter whether I study or not,' replied Rahul wearily. 'I have tried very hard. But I am just not cut out for the sciences.'

'And you have realized this now, during your exams?' asked Shweta sarcastically.

'I realized it long ago,' replied Rahul. 'You refused to listen to me. I tried my best,' he said flatly.

Rohit and Shweta fell silent.

Their daughter was missing and now their son had dropped this bombshell. Where had they gone wrong? Their perfect children did not seem perfect anymore. What would society say?

Then followed the agonizing period of waiting. Rohit was intermittently on the phone with the police commissioner. A few of their friends, colleagues and well-wishers dropped in to enquire and console them. Shweta was almost beside herself with worry. Rohit grew increasingly tense as the hours flew by.

Then, at 1 a.m., they received a phone call. Juhi had been located. The police had traced her and she would be brought home.

A number of thoughts crossed Shweta's mind. 'How? Where, what and why?' But she had to wait for her daughter.

After half an hour, the police brought Juhi.

Shweta ran towards her daughter and hugged her, crying loudly.

'Where did you go?' she questioned.

But Juhi remained silent. Something was different about her.

The officer cleared his throat and spoke to them. 'Sir, Ma'am. We found her in a flat in the outskirts of the city. Actually, we received a complaint from the society about a party and loud music. When we went to investigate, we found your daughter there. There were a number of teenagers there… and drugs were found.'

This announcement left Shweta and Rohit speechless. They looked at their daughter and realized that she was neither aware of her surroundings nor did she seem to care.

'When had she become like this?' they both wondered.

Rohit thanked the policemen after observing all formalities. After seeing the men off, Rohit and Shweta sat down to ponder. There was no point in asking their daughter anything at the moment. She was not in her senses. But how did such a situation come about with not one, but both their children? They did not understand their children. What happened to their perfect family? Had they ever been perfect?

If only they had not been so engrossed in their careers. If only they had spent some time with the children. If only they had not foisted their dreams and aspirations on the children. But it was not too late. Instead of pointing fingers at each other, the family would have to learn to work hard and rectify their mistakes.

Belief

Preeti had just turned thirty-five last week, but no one who looked at her would have thought so. She looked much older than her actual age. She was of medium height and was quite plump. Her face was still pretty, but it had become flabby. There were tyres of flab around her waist as well.

But her appearance hardly bothered her. She mostly donned sarees and occasionally salwar-kameez sets. Her forehead was always adorned with a huge bindi and the centre parting on her hair was full of sindoor, as if she had applied a full spoon. She had, more or less, dressed in the same manner for the past seventeen years.

Yes, it had been seventeen years since she had married Ram Nayak. She had not been a plump girl back then.

Preeti was a pretty college student, barely eighteen, when her father informed her that he had fixed her marriage with Ram Nayak. Preeti knew that her marriage would be an arranged one as her father did not believe in the concept of 'love marriages'. It was only that she had not expected it to happen so quickly after her eighteenth birthday.

She was an only child and her father was a very rich businessman. She knew that a lot of boys in her college were interested in her, but she had never been affected by the attention. She was a sensible girl and she thought that any feelings on her part would only bring her heartbreak. She was an average student and had no real ambitions, and so she readily agreed to her father's plans.

Ram Nayak was a rising politician. He was shrewd, astute and ambitious—all the qualities admired by Preeti's father, who had secretly always wanted a son to carry on the huge business empire that he had created, but Preeti turned out to be his only child; his wife could not conceive again. He then pinned his hopes on his daughter. But she was of average intelligence and her father had to accept that she would be unable to shoulder much responsibility. He did not lose hope. He decided to look for an intelligent son-in-law to fulfil his dreams.

This was how Ram Nayak was chosen.

Ram Nayak belonged to a respectable family and was from the same community as Preeti's family. He lived with his parents and had two other siblings. The only glitch in the plan was that he was a good twelve years older than his daughter. But Preeti's father reasoned that this was not a negative point. Didn't he have approximately the same age-gap with his own wife? And there were no problems in their marriage. So, he decided to ignore it and go ahead with the marriage.

Ram Nayak's family was overwhelmed by the proposal. As an upcoming politician, Ram Nayak quickly calculated his advantage and found that he was in a win-win situation. The only thing that he lacked was money, and with a rich father-in-law, he saw a lot of possibilities opening up. The girl was pretty, presentable and young, and he would be able to mould her to be a perfect wife for a politician like him. So he agreed to the proposal without much delay.

The marriage was solemnized with great pomp and splendour. Preeti enjoyed all the attention and stepped into her new home full of expectations. But from the very beginning, Ram Nayak laid down the rules of their marriage.

'Preeti,' he addressed her on their wedding night, 'you know I am a politician. I mostly remain in my constituency, looking after the welfare of my people. Hence do not expect me to be there by your side for every little thing,' he paused.

Preeti, who had romantic ideas, just stared back at him with her kohl-lined eyes.

'It is not that I do not care for you,' he reasoned softly, 'but my people have always been my priority. I know you are a very understanding girl and we will work this out.' He promised.

Preeti could do nothing but agree to his suggestion. She was determined to make her marriage work.

And so began Preeti's married life. Ram Nayak was loving and caring whenever he spent time with Preeti. He would shower her with expensive gifts. Preeti got along well with her in-laws. She was a practical girl and immersed herself in the management of her household. She was quite happy with the way things had turned out.

A couple of years passed, and then the usual whispers and questions started. 'When are they thinking of starting a family?' 'There is no use delaying things, Ram Nayak is already in his thirties.'

At first, Preeti brushed aside these queries. She, of course, conveyed all her concerns to her husband. But he was a busy man and did not quite pay her much attention. Another couple of years passed.

By now, Preeti was worried. Was something wrong with her? Why hadn't she conceived? She voiced her fears to her husband. He listened to her patiently. He asked her to visit the doctor. She argued that the problem might lie with him, but he brushed the possibility aside. Instead of arguing with him, Preeti went ahead and consulted the family doctor. What followed was a battery of tests and consultations. The verdict shocked Preeti. She could never conceive.

Preeti was greatly depressed by this turn of events; Ram Nayak, even more so. He turned to his work for solace, and in doing so, he had even less time for his wife. Her in-laws were very disappointed, but on seeing their daughter-in-law's plight, they did not display their grief.

Preeti thought about adopting a child. But neither her husband nor his family supported the idea. They vehemently opposed her.

Preeti was at her wit's end. She had very little to do apart from managing the house. She decided to speak to her husband about it. But when she broached the subject, her husband said, 'Why don't you go shopping? Or change the decor of the house? You have the luxury to go to spas or watch as many movies as you want! What else do you need?'

Making no headway, Preeti grew depressed. She had so much time on her hands, but no friends. And she was tired of the pitiful looks she received from her relatives. She had no wish to spend more time with them than necessary. She craved company and friendship. She thought of her school and college friends. But most of them either had demanding careers or were busy with their offsprings.

If only she had a child! She would shower him or her with love and affection, thought Preeti.

Preeti continued to go shopping or to the spa to break the monotony of her routine. It was at the spa that she bumped into her college friend, Reema. Reema looked young and beautiful and Preeti was surprised to see that she had not changed a bit. Reema, on the other hand, could hardly recognize Preeti. Her transformation, from a petite girl to a plump woman, was too much for Reema to comprehend.

Hiding her astonishment, Reema started chatting with Preeti about their mutual friends.

Preeti asked Reema, 'How do you know about so many of our friends? Have you kept in touch with them after college?'

Reema laughed and replied, 'It's Facebook that has made it possible. Aren't you on Facebook?' she asked.

Preeti shook her head. She had never been tech-savvy. Although she carried the latest iPhone, she mainly confined her usage to making and receiving calls; at times, she WhatsApped her husband and her family.

'Why, it's so easy!' said Reema. 'Let me download it for you,' she offered.

Preeti was only too happy to let her do it. Since Reema had the time to spare, she downloaded it for Preeti and opened a Facebook account for her, showing her how to go about it. Preeti was thrilled. They exchanged phone numbers and promised to be in touch.

Preeti was excited to be connected to all her friends. It had been so many years since she had communicated with them. Her friends were also happy to hear from her. They knew that she was married to a powerful politician, therefore, they had kept their distance. But when they found out that

Preeti was her same, old, simple self, they too reached out to her.

Preeti had a new purpose now. Her day started with Facebook and ended with it. She hardly noticed her husband's absence. Social media became an addiction for Preeti. She learnt a variety of things. It opened a whole new world to her. So much so, that she became active on Instagram and Twitter too.

It gave her new insights into fashion, latest news, controversies, and so many other things. She was grateful to Reema and she met her often at coffee shops or restaurants. They spent time chatting and gossiping. She was no longer depressed and her husband was relieved to see her old self.

But after about six months, Preeti became slightly bored. She wanted to get fit and decided to join a gym nearby. Ram Nayak was only too happy that his wife had found something else to focus on.

Preeti started going to the gym. At first, she was very self-conscious. But when she found that there were even more plumper ladies in the gym than herself, she became more confident. Being a friendly person, she interacted freely with others. She met a lot of people and enjoyed working out in the gym.

Preeti slimmed down a lot and started feeling good about herself. Her Facebook friends grew in number as she added a lot of gym-goers too. And then, there were friends of friends. She had so many friend requests! Initially, she had been cautious, but then she thought, 'If they want to be my friend what's the harm?' Slowly, the number of friends on her Facebook profile increased.

Meanwhile, the distance between Preeti and Ram Nayak

grew. They hardly spent any time together. Ram Nayak knew Preeti would always be there for him. He almost took her for granted. Preeti knew he was married to politics. He had spelled it out to her on the first day of their marriage.

And now, except for living in the same house, they hardly had anything in common. Rumour had it that Ram Nayak's party was planning to make him the president. Ram Nayak had also heard about it, and he was working even harder now.

Preeti was, of course, busy in her own world, blissfully unaware of these rumours. Her new routine was the gym, social media, shopping, spas and her friends. Her Facebook friends had now crossed an impressive three thousand mark. She sometimes even bragged about it to her friends. She loved their envious reactions.

On a Monday morning, Preeti went to the gym, as usual, and started her workout. After some time, she became aware of two or three groups leaving their usual workout and discussing something in earnest. She did not pay much heed to it and continued with her workout. When she finished, she saw that many people were still chatting in groups.

'What's the matter?' she asked a friend. But everyone she asked shook their head in denial.

Preeti thought that everyone was looking at her strangely, but she couldn't fathom the reason for it. Thinking that she had misread the situation, she walked out of the gym.

But when she reached home, she found a very angry Ram Nayak waiting for her.

'What is this?' he asked her angrily, flashing his cell phone.

'What is what?' said Preeti, bewildered.

'You don't know?' he asked her in a quiet and ominous tone.

Preeti shook her head, perplexed.

Ram Nayak opened his WhatsApp and showed her a number of photographs of Preeti, nude. The photographs were obscene and horrible.

Preeti was stunned and became speechless.

'How could this have happened?' she thought. She had never ever taken a nude photo of herself. What was happening?

She told her husband as much, but he was in no mood to listen. She had never seen him in such a towering rage. His cell phone started to ring. The landline number rang continuously.

She sat down, thunderstruck. She had not imagined the people at the gym; they had been looking at her strangely. They were actually curious. Oh god, what must her friends—or for that matter, everybody—be thinking of her? Would they believe that she was really capable of doing such things? She was mortified. How would she ever show her face to her friends? Or to her relatives?

She looked at her husband who was desperately trying to control the damage. Media reporters had now arrived at their residence. They behaved like a pack of wolves. They had sighted a prey and they were not likely to leave their residence without a juicy story. Her husband was speaking to the high command. The timing was wrong. He was explaining something desperately, but the person at the other end did not seem to want to hear him.

Ram Nayak sat down quietly. He suddenly seemed very old.

'They have rejected my name for president,' he stated flatly, his eyes devoid of expression. 'They cannot afford a scandal at this juncture—before the elections. All my hard work gone in a minute. 'Why, why did you do it?' he questioned his wife.

'I didn't do it,' she replied, already weary of the false accusation.

He looked at his wife. She looked bewildered. She had always been a good wife. Not demanding, always very understanding. She had never done anything to antagonize him. She could not do such a thing! No, it was simply not possible. She was a simple soul and innocent.

He was convinced. He had to get to the bottom of this sordid affair.

Who would target her? He had a lot of enemies in his field. Politics, as the saying went, was the last refuge of a scoundrel after all. But to do this to his wife? No, it had to be someone who wanted to settle scores with him.

He asked Preeti for her cell phone and she readily handed it over. He went to her Facebook account and started checking it. He was astounded to see the number of Facebook friends she had.

'Do you know all your Facebook friends personally?' he asked.

She shook her head silently.

He understood what had happened. After diligently searching through her account for a few minutes, he found what he was looking for. His rival Gopal Verma had done it. Gopal Verma's associate had befriended his gullible wife on Facebook and morphed her pictures.

He boiled with anger at the underhand means his rival had used. 'How could he stoop so low?' he thought.

But he went on to realize that Verma would do anything for power. He could go to any extent.

Then, he introspected. What had he given his wife? Oh, he had given her enough money and she lived in comfort.

But was that enough? He had not given her his valuable time. She was always fending for herself. And he could not protect her from this disrepute, even though she was not even guilty. He had been so busy with his constituency and other people that he had not stopped to even consider his wife's feelings.

Enough was enough, he thought. He would correct himself. He would fight this taint.

It would take time, he pondered. But then, he would not let his rival get away with this underhand deed. He was not just a politician but a seasoned one. The wrong would be corrected. This was the least he could do for his wife!

The Decision

Arup belonged to a middle-class family. His family consisted of his father, mother and his four elder brothers. His father was a hardworking farmer and his mother was a housewife. His brothers had done well academically and his parents were proud of their achievements. The eldest one was a doctor, the next brother was an engineer, followed by a lawyer, and the fourth brother was an architect.

Arup felt inadequate when he compared himself to his brothers. His performance in academics was poor. It took him two attempts to clear his tenth board examinations; he then took up commerce. This was also a wrong decision on his part as he could not clear his twelfth boards, not even in two attempts. His family had given up on him doing well academically. It was not that he did not try. But in comparison to his older brothers, he was a dullard.

Arup was very close to his mother as he was the youngest. He was pampered by her. But he was sick of the taunts of his older brothers and the other villagers. He had tried! He had really tried! But he just could not clear his boards. His friends and classmates had graduated. Everyone seemed to be doing so well. He also wanted to do something that his family and friends would be proud of. He was tired of being the butt of jokes for all and sundry. To be made fun of was indeed a horrible thing.

It was under these circumstances that he came into contact with a couple of older boys from his village. They belonged to a banned extremist organization. They were on the run and had come to visit their ailing mother for the night. The villagers knew about the visit. But since the villagers were a close-knit community, there was no fear of information being leaked to the army or police.

Curious, Arup started talking to them and asked them about their lives. Sensing an easy prey, the boys gave him a rosy picture of what they did. Arup listened with rapt attention, absorbing all that they had to say.

For the next two weeks, Arup was very quiet. He was continuously thinking. The boys from the banned organization had left the village, but they had deeply impacted Arup's thoughts. He had always wanted to do something different, something to make others notice him. This was not possible for him to achieve academically. He was always being compared to his illustrious brothers. He was a good sportsperson. But he did not have it in him to be at the top. He knew his limitations. What if he joined the banned organization? It would be for a good cause. He would be doing it for his motherland. His family and villagers would also not make fun of him! Yes, this was an idea he could explore.

The only issue was that he would have to leave his mother and stay away from his family. But he could always visit her once in a while.

Arup had made up his mind. But he was careful not

to reveal his plans to his family and friends. He knew that they would try to dissuade him from joining the organization as that path was fraught with danger. Nevertheless, he was excited about joining them, the dangers notwithstanding. So he quietly went about making his own arrangements. It took him six months to finally join the organization and leave home. He wrote a note to his mother stating his reasons and asked her not to worry.

Arup's decision shocked the family. The family were law-abiding citizens, and this step of Arup's was viewed very seriously. His mother was heartbroken and his father maintained stoic silence. The brothers were worried about the reputation of the family and the possible repercussions. But there was no way they could contact their younger brother and try to make him see reason. It took them some time to realize that they could simply do nothing about the situation.

Meanwhile, Arup, who was very enthusiastic about his new-found cause, was beginning to realize that life within the banned organization was not going to be smooth and easy.

First, he had to travel a long distance, cross the country's border clandestinely and train rigorously with other boys under the harsh conditions in the jungle. Meals in the jungle were frugal and he had to live a disciplined life. Once his training was complete, he had to come back to his country. But they always seemed to be on the run and never stayed at one place for too long and were always in small groups. Sometimes, his conscience troubled him. He was made to do things which he really did not want to do. There was no freedom and they had to act on the directives of the commanders. It seemed like such a long time had passed since he had left his village. And mostly, he missed his mother—her love and warmth.

Earlier, he had thought that he would visit her from time to time, whenever it was possible. But now, he found out that it was impossible to do so. They were always on the run and had to be alert.

Then came the big assignment. The organization was planning a big act of terror to show their strength. A number of bombs were to be planted in the big city. Arup was, however, assigned to plant a bomb in the town near his village, as he knew the area well. He had misgivings about the whole act. In his heart of hearts, he did not really approve of these acts. But the members had all been taught that it was for the greater good. So he tried to reconcile himself to the situation.

On the given date, Arup, along with his accomplice Rajen, rode to the market on an old scooter. Their job was simple. They just had to leave the scooter with the bomb in the marketplace. The timer had been adjusted in a way that the blast would take place a couple of hours later. And by that time, they would be far away.

'Rajen, are you sure there won't be any police checks?' questioned Arup for the umpteenth time.

'Nah,' replied Rajen confidently. 'They don't check on weekly market days.'

Arup was quiet after that. He hoped that the casualties would be low. But the worrying factor was that it was a weekly market day. So people from nearby villages thronged the market. There would be people from his village too.

The two cadres of the banned organization parked the scooter in the marketplace and quietly walked away. They caught a bus to their next destination, which was seven hours away. After the bus had travelled for an hour or so, Arup breathed a sigh of relief. Now they were relatively safe.

They reached their destination in the evening. Arup wanted to know about the outcome of their deed. He urged their hosts to switch on the television to enable him to watch the 7 p.m. news.

The organization had wreaked havoc. Television channels were displaying heart-wrenching scenes. The number of casualties were very high and kept increasing. Arup watched the television in silence. There were angry reactions from the general public. He watched the politicians who were trying to placate the general public. The big city had borne the brunt of the explosions. There were eighty-seven casualties. The other small towns had few other casualties.

Arup then saw the result of his particular misdeed. Twelve people had lost their lives. Three women and nine men, including two children. He was sickened by what he had done.

They were displaying pictures of the dead with their names. He was about to turn away when the picture on the display caught his eye.

Sonmai Bora, it read. Yes. It was his mother's picture. He watched in shock and disbelief. His heart skipped a beat. His mouth went dry.

'It couldn't be! How could it be?' Arup thought, dazed. 'There must be some mistake.'

He could not sleep the whole night. He kept watching the news channels till late in the night. Rajen could not understand that something was amiss. Early in the morning, Arup waited for the newspaper. Yes, it was on the front page. The gory details and the names of the victims. He had killed his mother with one thoughtless act. He had killed the only person who had loved him for himself. How would he be able to live with that? It was too high a price to pay for one wrong decision.

Deity

Revati looked at the report in her hand and sighed. She was troubled and tired, whereas she should have felt elated. But this was the third time.

She had been married for three years now and hers was an arranged marriage. Her father was very happy to have her married into an aristocratic family. He had gone through a lot of trouble to arrange the marriage. He had wanted the best for his daughter, like all loving fathers do. Suraj was a loving husband and a perfect partner. They lived in a joint family. Her husband was the youngest among five brothers. He was well-educated. After completing his MBA abroad, he had joined the family business.

Revati too was well-educated, but she did not work. Two of her sisters-in-law were working in colleges, but she preferred to be a homemaker. She wanted to be there for her children when they were born; she wanted to be a hands-on mother and watch them grow. She wanted to pamper them and be the best mother. But that was when she had just been married and had rosy dreams.

During the first year of her marriage, she discovered she was pregnant. Elated, she shared the news with her husband, who, in turn, shared it with his family. Revati was then taken to the family doctor. The doctor examined her and did a sonography. He then announced that the baby was going to be a girl.

Immediately her in-laws went into a huddle. Then, her mother-in-law told her bluntly that she would have to abort the baby. Revati was shocked! She could not comprehend the turn of events. She was not even asked for her opinion or her desire. Before she even realized what was happening, she was made to abort the child. The enormity of what she had to go through struck her when she reached home. She could not eat or sleep properly for two days. Her husband could not console her and decided to send her home for a few days.

Her family was shocked to see her.

'Why, Ma?' questioned Revati listlessly.

Her mother consoled her. Her father was also grief-stricken. He had only wanted to see her happy.

Revati went back to her in-laws after twenty days. No one mentioned the abortion. It was as though her unborn child was a forgotten chapter.

But Revati questioned her husband. 'Why didn't you stop them?'

Suraj bowed his head, not meeting her eyes. 'You know that my father takes all the major decisions in this family. For three generations, there has been no girl child born in this family. And he would like to continue the tradition.'

Revati looked at her husband in disbelief. She was astounded by the patriarchal explanation. She knew that there was no point arguing. So she kept her thoughts to herself.

In her second year of the marriage, Revati found herself pregnant again. She was afraid to disclose it to her husband and her in-laws, but she knew she had no option. Her worst fears came true, and she had to undergo an abortion for the second time. She went through feelings of guilt and remained depressed for a long time.

Her husband was sympathetic, but there was very little he could do. Her in-laws went about their daily business as though nothing had happened.

Somehow, Revati reconciled herself with the fact that she had lost two children. She went about her daily routine as usual, but the happy, bubbly girl was now a pale shadow of herself. Her dreams were shattered. She could not talk about her feelings with anyone. She tried to broach the subject with Suraj, but apart from sympathy, he was clueless. He understood her feelings and tried to give her time. But he did not have answers about what would happen if the next baby was a girl too.

Revati did not want to become pregnant again and go through the same trauma. But fate willed otherwise.

She read over her report. It said she was pregnant again.

This time, she did not reveal her pregnancy to anyone. Not even to her husband. She decided to come up with a strategy. But what could she do? She thought and thought, but couldn't come up with a solution. She was at her wit's end.

That night, when the whole family sat down for dinner, Revati suddenly went off into a trance. She started speaking in a different voice. Her husband was startled, and went towards her, full of concern. He tried to touch her arms, but she shook him off, angrily.

'Stay away from me,' she shrieked in a high-pitched tone. 'Listen to me,' she said menacingly, rolling her eyes maniacally. 'I have come to your family for a reason. Let the time come. I will disclose it all.'

Revati's body was moving and jerking. It was a terrifying sight to behold. Her hair was open and she was muttering to herself. This continued for a good ten minutes. Then, she suddenly went limp and laid down, senseless.

Her in-laws were terrified. What was happening? They could not fathom it. Suraj was sprinkling water on Revati. She moaned as she was slowly coming to her senses.

Her mother-in-law said, 'I will call her parents right now. They have cheated us and hidden facts,' she said indignantly.

She immediately called up Revati's parents. They were surprised. They kept reiterating that nothing like this had ever happened before. Revati's in-laws were not convinced.

Meanwhile, gaining consciousness, Revati sat down, looking bewildered.

'What happened?' she asked her husband.

'You seriously don't remember?' he questioned.

'Remember what?' asked Revati, puzzled.

'Okay,' said Suraj, 'Just relax.'

Revati was taken to her bedroom. She was asked to rest.

The family then sat down for a discussion. Everyone had different points of view. Finally, after intensive talks, it was decided that Revati would be taken to the hospital for an overall body check-up.

The next day, Revati went to the hospital, accompanied by her husband and her mother-in-law. Revati's mother-in-law explained the problem to the doctor privately. The doctor then put her through a battery of tests. Revati's pregnancy was discovered, so was the gender of her baby. Revati's worst fears were confirmed! But this time, the doctor declined to abort the baby immediately. Her mother-in-law tried to convince the doctor that it was best for her daughter-in-law to abort as she had violent fits and may not be in a healthy state to carry her baby. She said that the baby might already have come to harm. But the doctor could not be convinced to carry out the abortion.

Revati went home, relieved. During the next three weeks, she had two more 'fits'. Her in-laws panicked and started consulting godmen, astrologers and soothsayers. Most of them opined that she was possessed by a deity.

Now this posed a huge dilemma for the family. Word had spread in the society that Revati was possessed by a deity. There was always a queue of visitors at the door. Some came to pay obeisance; some were curious to see her. The doctor still refused to abort the baby. Revati's in-laws had to reconcile themselves to the fact that they would not be able to get rid of the baby.

Afraid of the consequences that may befall them, they decided to appease the goddess by pampering Revati. The next few months were amazing for Revati. All of her wishes and demands were met.

She even had her 'fits' a few more times.

Finally, after a few months, Revati delivered a healthy baby girl. Her in-laws were in awe of the baby and welcomed her with great pomp and splendour.

Revati now knew her baby daughter was finally safe. When she went home with her baby, the first thing she did was light a diya for her deity. She begged forgiveness for using the deity to protect her unborn baby, but there was no other option left for her. She thanked the mother goddess for not exposing her lies and helping her with the plan. The mother goddess had blessed her indeed.

Divine Justice

Deben was sipping tea at the roadside vendor on the corner of the street. It was evening and the street was busy. Buses and cars were piled, bumper to bumper; two-wheelers and commuters were all in a hurry to get back home. Everyone seemed to be in a hurry. After all, it was a Friday. Wives were waiting for their husbands, children and those who were single were waiting to either get out of the city for the weekend or party with their friends. Two days of holiday awaited all of them.

But there seemed to be no respite for Deben. He frowned at his predicament. His face was creased with worry. It had nearly been three years now since he had realized his mistake. He had tried to find solutions. But there seemed to be none.

He had always been a hard worker and an honest person. He thought of his simple wife, Sagarika. He rarely saw her smile these days. She was also stressed. His three young children were unaware of the issues their parents were going through. How was he going to look after their needs? He could barely make ends meet. He was already above forty.

One wrong decision had ruined their lives. Sometimes

he felt like ending his life…but that would be an easy way to escape. His family would have to bear the brunt. No, he would not do that. There had to be another way.

He rued the day he had met Kishore. Kishore had told him about this big company where he had invested his money. He had apparently gotten back thrice the amount he had invested in a very short time. Kishore had then become an agent for the company and was urging Deben to invest in the scheme. Deben was a plumber and was good at his work; he constantly had enough work on his hands. At times, he would be roped in by big contractors for major projects and he earned well. Deben was doing quite well for himself and when it came to money, he was always cautious.

However, he had found out that many of his friends and relatives had invested in Kishore's company and had got back rich dividends. This made him think. He decided to try his luck with a small amount. He was apprehensive at first, but within six months, he got back thrice the amount he had invested.

This was enough to convince him. Deben invested all his savings into the scheme the next time. He also became an agent for the company, just like Kishore, and started working for the company. He persuaded many people to invest their money in the scheme, bringing in investments worth about ₹20 lakh from other people.

But after eight months, one morning, his world came crashing down.

The Central Bureau of Investigation had raided the company; it was found that a huge amount had been collected from the lower middle-class people, and the owners had fled the country. There was connivance on the part of the politicians, police and bureaucrats. The personnel manning the offices of the company were picked up by the police for questioning. Those running the offices were arrested.

There were huge crowds outside the offices. Everyone wanted their money back and the people who had invested had several questions. But there were no answers.

Deben could not believe it at first. Slowly, he had come to accept it. He had lost all his savings. He had put all his eggs in one basket, and the result was that he had no savings now. He was numb with shock and the shock slowly turned to despair.

But there was worse to come.

People began queuing up in front of his house. They wanted their money back. They would not listen to reason. Deben felt trapped. He had been instrumental in persuading people to invest in the company, and the people were now beginning to hound him for their money. He had no means to get back the amount he had invested in the company. So how could he get back the money that belonged to other people? He tried to explain that he too was a victim. But they were not willing to see reason.

Deben's life was a living hell. He was an honest person. He could not bear the fact that his mistake had led to such suffering. He and his family suffered abuses and curses from relatives and friends who had invested their money as well. The shame and misery were too much to bear.

But he knew he had to be strong. The only thing that kept him going was his firm faith in god. He had always been an honest, hard-working man. There had to be a way out of this mess! god would surely help him.

For three years, Deben struggled. He still found no

solution. The police picked him up for questioning on and off. It was a matter of disgrace for him that he was considered to have committed a crime. But the police too realized that he was a victim. Deben was relieved that the police had understood the situation. The other people who had invested through Deben were soon resigned to their fate.

Finishing his customary evening tea, Deben paid the vendor and slowly joined the other commuters on the pavement. It was a long walk home. As Deben turned a corner, he felt something fall against his arms. As he looked to see what had hit him, he found a bundle of two-thousand-rupee notes. He picked it up slowly and looked up to find a few more bundles raining down from the building. There were two or three other people there as well. They were busy grabbing the bundles of money. Deben, too, joined them. He collected a few bundles and put it inside his bag. He looked up and saw that the top floor of the building was brightly lit up.

He was puzzled.

The other people picked up the money and quickly disappeared. He looked around and found a few more bundles of money. Picking them up, he walked away at a fast pace. He quickened his pace and did not stop until he reached home.

On reaching home, he asked his wife for a glass of water. Then he closed the bedroom door and opened his bag. He carefully started counting the money. The total amount, as it turned out, was eight lakh and fifty thousand rupees. He could not believe it.

But he did not disclose this to anyone.

After dinner, he went to sleep.

Deben did not sleep soundly that night. He tossed and turned. Where had the money come from? Was it god? It was more money than what he had invested. What should be his next step? Should he try to return the money? But who would he return the money to? He did not even know whom the money belonged to. What was he supposed to do? With these troubled thoughts, Deben fell asleep in the early hours of the morning.

When he woke up the next day, the sun was already high in the sky. His wife made him a cup of tea.

'Have you heard what happened yesterday?' questioned Sagarika.

'What?' asked Deben curiously.

'Yesterday, in Lindsay Street, the house of Mittals was raided by the CBI. The newspapers say that they threw money out of their window of their flat in fear of being detected,' she ended.

'Mittals?' questioned Deben.

'Yes,' replied Sagarika. 'The ones who were running the new chit fund company,' she explained.

Deben was stunned. He had lost all his money to a chit fund group who had duped him. He had again received money from the owners of another chit fund company who were duping other poor people. It seemed like a story. But it did not feel right to keep the money. He pondered over the matter for a long time. Finally, he decided to go to the local police station and confess about how he had come to have the money.

'So what brings you to the police station?' asked Mr Chatterjee, the station house officer.

Deben explained everything in detail and confessed to receiving the money.

'Just give me a lakh and keep the rest,' said Mr Chatterjee with a wink.

'But, but...' protested Deben.

'It's okay. The matter will remain between us. Think of it as a gift from god,' said Mr Chatterjee.

Deben walked out of the police station in a daze. He would keep the money and share it with his relatives and friends who had lost their money. There was no other explanation. It was divine justice.

Hope

Mr and Mrs Kaushik Sharma lived in Guwahati. Mr Sharma worked at Guwahati University as an assistant professor in the department of physics. Mrs Sharma worked at the Kendriya Vidyalaya where she taught economics. Mr Sharma had been allotted a house with a small compound by the university. The location of the house was quite convenient as Mr Sharma had to walk for less than five minutes to reach his department; Mrs Sharma too would go to school, a ten-minute ride from home, on the school bus. School ended by 2 p.m. and Mrs Sharma would reach home by 2.30 p.m. or so. Mr Sharma would finish his classes by 3 p.m. It was a very satisfactory arrangement for both of them.

After a couple of years, Mrs Sharma conceived her first child. She continued working at the school until the child was born. She was blessed with a beautiful baby boy and the Sharmas named him Gautam. But as Mrs Sharma had received only three months of maternity leave, she desperately looked for help to look after the little one. She tried to hire a couple of women, but they were unsuitable as she did not find them reliable. She discussed the matter with her husband, but they could not find a solution. Her in-laws were too old to live with them and look after the baby; her own parents had to look after her two younger siblings who were still in college.

So after a lot of thought, she came to a decision. She would leave her job. She had to leave her job for the well-being of her little child and so, Mrs Sharma became a housewife. She was so busy with her household chores and looking after her son that she didn't miss her job. Very soon, it was time for Gautam to attend school himself.

From day one, she resolved to teach Gautam herself. Now that he was going to school, Mrs Sharma had time for herself. She finished all her chores, and in the evening, she taught Gautam his lessons. Gautam was a bright boy and he learned quickly; he topped his class since primary school.

The Sharmas soon had big dreams for their only child. They showered him with attention and he was rewarded for his good results with a short vacation or books.

As Gautam grew, he slowly realized the difference between him and the other boys. Boys his age had lots of friends, played various sports together or involved themselves in other activities. Gautam was not allowed to play games or learn music. He did not even spend time with other boys after school hours. He had to go home, rest and study. It became a bit monotonous for him. He was only allowed to take part in debates and quiz competitions.

'But why, Ma?' asked Gautam in frustration one day.

'Because sports in India will not lead you anywhere unless you are very good,' replied his mother. 'And music will not sustain you.'

Gautam thought about it. He did not want to play sports

or learn music to make it a profession. But his parents would hear none of it.

In fact, when he was in his teens his grades slipped due to such thoughts. He did not top the class, but came third. His parents were alarmed. They could not believe it. Where had they gone astray? This wouldn't do at all. Something was seriously wrong.

The Sharmas started to monitor their son more than usual. Gautam was a hardworking boy, but he started to work even harder. His parents wanted him to study in IIT; they did not ask him what he wanted to do. They wanted their son to shine. It was as though they were forcing their ambitions onto him. They wanted him to achieve heights that they never could. So although Gautam loved humanities and poetry, he was compelled to pursue science to attain the objective of his parents. Gautam passed his twelfth board exams with flying colours and also cleared his IIT entrance examination. He went on to study at IIT Kharagpur. Even before he had completed his engineering degree, he got a job in America at a prestigious company through campus recruitment. So after completing his course, Gautam left for America, the land his parents had always dreamt that he would work in.

Gautam joined his new job and settled in, adjusting well to the new place. His parents were sad that their only son would be living so far away, but they were also proud of his achievement. They reasoned that they could always visit him from time to time and vice versa.

Meanwhile, Gautam was beginning to enjoy his new-found freedom. Even while studying in IIT, and though he had stayed in a hostel, he always made studies his priority. He did not really enjoy any freedom as such. But America was different. He went to work; after that, he was free to do as he pleased for the first time in his life. Weekends were, of course, the best. He indulged in so many activities. He made a few friends and loved his life in the new country. He called his parents dutifully every week.

In this manner, nearly a year passed. Mr Sharma had a sudden stroke on the way to his class. He was immediately taken to a nearby hospital. He survived, but the left side of his body was paralysed. The days were traumatic for Mrs Sharma. Gautam came home immediately upon receiving the news, but he could only stay for three weeks. Mrs Sharma had to cope on her own thereafter. She understood her son's compulsions, but for the first time, she wished that he lived nearer to his parents.

Mr Sharma became bedridden. Gautam supported his parents financially and continued his weekly calls, but he could only come home once a year. There was not much that he could do from such a distance. Mr Sharma retired from service and the Sharmas shifted to their own house. Mrs Sharma now devoted her time to looking after her husband.

Meanwhile, Gautam fell in love with an American girl. After a few months, he married the girl and broke the news to his parents. He knew they would not approve of his wife. This news came as a bolt from the blue for his parents. They could not believe that their obedient, dutiful son would take such a major step and they felt that they had lost 'control' of their only son.

They ranted and raved about their fate. But nothing could be done. They had no option.

Gautam came to visit home with his American wife. His parents were cold towards her and this angered Gautam. His wife found India hot and humid and could not adjust to the weather. The attitude of her in-laws towards her was the final straw; she resolved to never come back to India.

Gautam was dismayed by the turn of events, but he could understand his wife's strong feelings. He, too, did not have positive feelings when it came to his parents because of his restricted childhood. As a result, he grew apart from his parents. After he went back to America, Gautam's phone calls to his parents were few and far between.

After a couple of years, Gautam's wife gave birth to twins. This news brought happiness to the Sharmas. They longed to see their grandchildren. Gautam first made the excuse that the children were too young to travel. But after a few years, it became obvious that Gautam was unwilling to bring his new family over to his parents. However, Gautam visited his parents alone for a brief period every couple of years.

During his last visit, Gautam noticed that the strain of looking after his father was taking a toll on his mother. She was starting to forget things. She kept repeating sentences and asked him the same questions. He took her to the doctor and she was diagnosed with the early stages of dementia. There was nothing he could do for her. He could not take them back to America with him.

After six months, Gautam's father had another stroke. He did not survive. Gautam rushed back to India again and completed the last rites like a dutiful son. He contemplated his mother's situation and then he made a decision.

The day before he left India, he packed his mother's belongings and left her at an old age home. He could not take her back with him. It would complicate his life.

Mrs Sharma still sits near the window of her room

overlooking the gate of the old age home. She has only one thought: her Gautam will come back to take her with him some day. Gautam...he will come...someday.

Learning

Rajiv was the only son of Mr and Mrs Vikram Pandey. As a close-knit middle-class family, they left no stone unturned to provide Rajiv with the best education and facilities. Both his parents worked in a bank. He had a happy childhood, but he was slightly spoiled as he did not see the sacrifices his parents made to give him the best of everything.

Rajiv was a brilliant student and his parents were full of pride at his achievements. He secured a seat in the prestigious IIT Kharagpur and graduated with flying colours. After that, he went to America for higher studies. But contrary to his parents' expectations, he came back to India to work in a multinational company in New Delhi. He met a woman there after joining the job. Ruchi, too, worked in the same company. So, within a year they were married with the blessings of their respective families.

Rajiv and Ruchi continued to live in Delhi after their marriage, working in the same office. Life was hectic for them. They attended tours, conferences, meetings, presentations, met friends, hosted parties and went on yearly vacations. Soon, Ruchi conceived. Their joy knew no bounds. Rajiv did everything possible to make Ruchi comfortable, and Ruchi revelled in the extra care and attention that Rajiv gave her.

In due course, Ayush was born. The Pandeys were overjoyed. Ruchi was on maternity leave for six months and she looked after Ayush. She was a doting mother. After four months Ruchi began to worry. Who would look after her son while she was at work? Rajiv brushed aside her fears and assured her that they would find help. But finding help did not come easy. Finally, they settled on a middle-aged lady to take care of Ayush after a round of interviews. Ruchi got back to work after her mandatory period of leave had ended.

The moment Ruchi joined work, she grew busy again. She struggled to balance work and home. She was also filled with guilt for having to leave the baby with her maid for long hours. She discussed her feelings with Rajiv, but he brushed them aside. But then, after a couple of months, the maid did not want to continue working for them. Ruchi became frantic. She took a leave for a few days. Her boss was unhappy as she was in the midst of an important project. It was a crisis.

Rajiv decided to ask his parents for help. Ruchi's parents were still working at a college and so it would not be possible for them to come and stay in Delhi. But Rajiv's parents had retired from service. He told them about the problems they were having with maids and Ruchi's worries. Mr and Mrs Pandey immediately agreed to come. Ruchi was relieved.

So, the Pandeys came to stay with their only son and his family. They were happy to help out in every little way. Rajiv and Ruchi, too, knew that their son would be well cared for. Ruchi could finally concentrate on her work. The Pandeys, too, felt needed and happy. It was a win-win situation for everyone.

And it was in such a loving atmosphere that little Ayush

grew up. Rajiv soon suggested that his parents sell the house that they owned in Chandigarh. His father was reluctant at first; it had been built with a lot of care with their hard-earned money. But Rajiv prevailed upon them, stating that there was no point in maintaining another property when they would be living together. So after some thought, the Pandeys sold their property in Chandigarh.

In the meantime, Ayush grew up and started attending school. He went to school early in the morning and came back in the afternoon. After a brief nap, he went to art classes and played sports. The Pandeys had more time for leisure. They had a few friends in the colony and met them from time to time.

But slowly, Mr Pandey began to suffer from heart ailments. They were ageing and it was but natural that they would develop maladies. Mrs Pandey suffered from high blood pressure and diabetes as well.

'Don't you think your parents are falling ill too frequently?' questioned Ruchi.

'What do you mean?' countered Rajiv. 'They are not doing it on purpose,' he defended.

But Rajiv too began to think about it. Trips to the doctors were becoming frequent. His father even had to be hospitalized for a few days as a pacemaker had to be implanted. Expenses were mounting. Of course, his parents had their pension and some money after selling their property in Chandigarh, but he could hardly ask them to spend their own money under the circumstances. He had also bought a big flat in a posh locality recently. So he had to consider his own loan as well. And his son was now attending an expensive school. They were planning to send him to an exclusive boarding school soon as well. Ruchi, too, had always been extravagant. She earned well, but she also spent it on herself. Rajiv had always been indulgent when it came to Ruchi's whims and fancies, so he couldn't change now. All he could do was hope for the best.

But this was not to be. After a couple of months, Mrs Pandey fell down during her morning walk and broke her hip bone. She had to undergo a surgery and the doctor informed Rajiv that his mother's bones had become brittle and that she was suffering from osteoporosis.

When Mrs Pandey came home, they had to hire nurses to look after her as they were told that she would be bedridden for some time. Now this was an added complication.

'Look, Rajiv,' said Ruchi, 'we brought your parents here to look after Ayush. But now we need extra help to look after your mother. They are really becoming a burden,' she grumbled selfishly.

Rajiv was quiet. He was torn between his obligation to his parents and his desire to keep his wife happy. He could not send his parents back to Chandigarh as the property had already been sold, but his house now resembled a mini-hospital. What was he to do?

Things continued in this manner for a couple of months and Ruchi continued with her complaints.

'You are always on tours. So I have to face the brunt,' she accused Rajiv.

Rajiv was silent. He was powerless when Ruchi was on a tirade. He did not know how to handle the situation. The worst part was that Ruchi's attitude towards his parents had changed considerably. She had become rude and overbearing.

The Pandeys, too, noticed the perceptible difference in their daughter-in-law. While she had never really been very loving or thoughtful, she had always been courteous. They also noticed that their son had become distant and abrupt. The household was no longer a happy one.

The Pandeys felt hurt and helpless at this turn of events. They rued the fact that they had sold their property. They did not have anyone to turn to. The elderly couple discussed the issue, considered all perspectives and tried to find a solution. They did not want to get in the way of their only child's happiness. Since it was a family matter, they did not feel that it was right to ask for advice from their friends and relatives.

Slowly, the situation in the house was becoming unbearable. The Pandeys, after much deliberation, came to a decision. They called their son and daughter-in-law and told them that after a lot of thought they had come to the conclusion that they would shift to an old age home. This would not burden Rajiv's family and in their old age, they too would be properly looked after.

Rajiv was dumbstruck at the solution. But he realized it was not a bad proposition. Ruchi was, of course, delighted with the decision. This would be wonderful for them. She would be getting rid of her in-laws, which she had been hoping to do for the past one year. Rajiv and Ruchi were both selfish. Now that the elderly Pandeys had outlived their utility, they no longer wanted them in their lives.

They set about in right earnest looking for an old age home that would be suitable as per all of them. After a lot of deliberations, they settled on one not very far from their home. The Pandeys felt sad that their only son had no compunctions about putting them in an old age home. They realized that it was their upbringing that was at fault. They had given him everything that he had wished for. As a result, he had become selfish and only thought about his own needs and wants. He could not see the pain and heartache that he was putting his parents through. They resigned themselves to their fate.

The Pandeys decided to move away at the beginning of the next month; there was no reason to delay their departure. They packed their meagre belongings and were ready to move.

Rajiv and Ruchi had both taken a leave from their office to settle the Pandeys into the old age home.

Ayush had also not gone to school. He was watching the baggage being loaded onto the vehicles with interest. Finally, when they were about to board the car, he understood that his grandparents were leaving his house for good. He was very attached to his grandparents and did not like the move. He objected vehemently.

Rajiv and Ruchi tried to gently explain everything to Ayush who listened to their reasons with rapt attention, and questioned them.

'I understand,' said Ayush finally. 'When both of you grow old and sick, I too will have to leave you in an old age home,' he said.

There was a shocked silence. Rajiv and Ruchi were taken aback at their son's observation.

'Isn't that so?' questioned Ayush.

His parents did not know how to respond. His grandparents were also silent.

Ruchi thought about what her son had just said. What were they teaching him? He would learn by the example his parents were setting. Her son, in his own innocent way, had shown her the folly of their actions. No, she could not let this happen. She had to stop this here and now.

'Let's abandon this idea,' she said.

'We will continue living together,' she finally announced.

Precious Moments

Maya was sitting with a cup of tea, gazing at the beautiful lawn outside her bungalow. Her thoughts strayed far away.

'Have I done the right thing?' she asked herself for the hundredth time.

But as she analysed, she felt no guilt. Something so beautiful could not be wrong, particularly when it felt so right. Instead, she felt liberated and also at peace with herself after so many years. She did not care that she had broken societal norms or that she would be judged by people. At this moment, her thoughts were only about herself, of feeling loved and wanted by another human being. Feelings that she thought she had lost long ago. She felt alive and happy after a long, long time.

Maya had married Aveek twenty years ago. Hers had been a fairy-tale romance, straight out of romantic novels that she had been constantly immersed in during her teens. The first few years had been blissful; then came along two children within a couple of years. Looking after the children had been a full-time job. She was a hands-on mother and cared for the children entirely, despite having a domestic help around. She was a loving wife and looked after the house well.

In fact, Aveek's friends too envied him for the lovely house that was well kept, his perfect children and his beautiful and doting wife.

A decade passed and the children got busy at school. Aveek was engrossed in his business, and slowly, the distance between the couple grew. At first, it was business trips, short ones, and then as the business grew, so did the duration of the visits. Of course, there were family vacations too. Initially in India, and then in exotic locales. It became a ritual every year, and the children looked forward to these trips.

Maya loved these trips. For her, it meant spending quality time with her family and shopping. She would bring back curios from these trips and it would occupy the pride of place in her display area in the living room. She loved to look at the reactions of her friends after seeing them there.

Slowly, as the years passed, she realized that her children were growing up and no longer came to her with their every need. Both of them were doing well academically and had varied interests. At times, she felt that the children were growing away from her and that they no longer needed her. But this was the rule of the universe. She tried to busy herself with charity work, her friends and the house. Aveek, too, spent less time with her these days. Whenever he was at home, he was either busy on his laptop or his phone, or he was too tired to speak to her. In fact, she tried but couldn't remember the last time she had had a decent conversation with Aveek or spent time with him.

Then the bombshell struck them. That was five years ago. As usual, the wife was the last to know. Aveek had been having an affair with his secretary for the last couple of years.

The business trips had not always been business trips. More often, business trips were combined with pleasure trips. Her world had shattered. It was as though she had been wrenched apart by this revelation.

Her mind was reeling with thoughts. 'How have I been so blind? Why didn't I notice the tell-tale signs? Have I been so busy and engrossed with my life that I failed to realize that we have slowly grown apart? It is all my fault. Or is it? Have I not been a good wife and an ideal mother to his children? When did the romance die?' These questions kept haunting her again and again.

Then came the anger at the betrayal. She decided to confront him and convey her feelings. But when she finally confronted Aveek, she was taken aback by his reaction. Instead of denying it, he admitted to the affair. He almost flaunted the affair, telling her that she bored him now and that there had been other affairs too.

She could not believe her ears. Was this really her Aveek saying such things to her? She was speechless.

He then told her that they were together only because he cared about the children. If she wanted, she could separate. He knew she had nowhere to go. Her parents had died a few years ago and she had no siblings. The worst part was that as a housewife she was economically dependent on him.

Where would she go? What would she do? She could take the children with her but that would deprive them of what was rightfully theirs. All these thoughts kept haunting her for the next few days. 'No.' She had decided. She would not leave Aveek. That would give him what he wanted. She needed time, time to think about a strategy. Yes, this was a war. A war within herself.

Slowly, she began to immerse herself in more work at the charity. Those few hours, when she was at the NGO for destitute women, served her like a balm. She worked hard and not a soul knew about the agony that raged within her. At home, she tried to keep things normal for the sake of her children. But she could not bear to share the same room with Aveek. It was only for her children that she was tolerating the situation, she told herself.

It was during this time that she met Kabir. He was a good ten years younger to her and had joined the NGO where she was working. His sincerity and zeal for the work attracted her. He was a handsome man in his mid-thirties and friendly by nature. He worked for long hours with a passion few could match. It was these qualities that drew her towards Kabir initially.

As they both spent long hours at the NGO, it was natural that they started spending more time together. Gradually, she started looking forward to that time. He was so easy to converse with and she found herself opening up to him. They would speak about everything, voicing their opinions freely. He was also perceptive to her different moods. He could sense the deep underlying unhappiness within her, but he did not try to probe further to find out about the cause. He respected her feelings.

Kabir was also married. He had two small children and a loving wife. Maya knew about them, and although she was attracted to him, she tried to keep her feelings under wraps. Kabir, too, had his share of domestic problems. A sick brother, an unemployed brother and an unmarried sister.

It pained her to see him grappling with these problems. She wanted him to be happy. He shared his problems with her from time to time over a cup of coffee or between breaks. Slowly, she too started sharing her personal feelings with him. She would pour out her heart to him and he would listen to her with his dark, intense eyes. No questions, no comments and no judgements.

They were comfortable in each other's company. They were friends, and yet, so much more. Sometimes even words were not necessary. They understood each other so well. A look, a smile, a gesture—and feelings were communicated. It was almost like they were soulmates with some cosmic connection.

Maya could not understand how and when she had developed such feelings for Kabir. She tried to remind herself that Kabir could never be hers. But the attraction was so strong that she could not help but spend as much time as she could with him. There were days when she thought she was no different from her husband. After all, she was attracted to a married man. She had never even looked at another man during her married life. And here she was, attracted to Kabir, who was a good ten years younger to her! It was totally unthinkable. Something was wrong with her.

'Not something, everything,' she thought despairingly.

She tried to stay away from the NGO and Kabir for a few days. She switched off her cell phone and stayed at home. She watched movies, went out for dinner with her friends, arranged the house and did everything possible to forget Kabir. She even tried to pray. But it was as if thoughts of Kabir had invaded every cell of her body. Unconsciously, her thoughts would wander back to him.

After trying to forget Kabir for a few days, unsuccessfully, Maya decided to go back to work. The moment she was back at the NGO, it was as though she had never been away, not even for a day. One look and a smile from Kabir and all her resolve to stay away from him disappeared.

It was no use fighting her feelings, she thought.

Kabir did not question her about her absence nor did he say that he missed her. But his actions conveyed his feelings to her. They worked quietly, side by side, not saying much, content to be in each other's company.

Their co-workers left, and they continued to work like before, long past their normal working hours. And then, it was time to leave for home. They were reluctant to do so, in spite of being in each other's company for the whole day. No words were spoken, and yet both of them knew. He looked at her with a question, and the answer was shining in her eyes. He reached out to her and she eagerly went into his arms.

'No,' she thought as she came to a conclusion. 'This isn't wrong. How can anything this beautiful ever be wrong?' she wondered.

She knew that this relationship would not last. He had too many commitments and she too could not come out in the open for the sake of the children, her family and society. But she knew that in the years to come, the love that she felt during those fleeting moments would be cherished by her forever. Because it had made her feel wanted, loved and beautiful; it had made her feel like a woman.

And those precious moments were enough to last her a lifetime.

Reflection

It was Rajiv Verma's last day at the office. Having achieved what he believed to be the pinnacle of success, he was now retiring from his job. He was the Chief Secretary of the state after a tenure of two years. He had put in thirty-seven years of service, and as he sat down at the farewell meeting that had been arranged for him, he thought about his past. He was very happy with all that he had achieved.

The next morning, Verma woke up a little late. He was relaxed and in a happy mood. He went to the dining room for breakfast and found the house quiet.

'Where is everybody?' he questioned his cook.

'Madam has gone out with her friends for the day. Baba has gone to work, and Baby to college,' replied the cook.

Verma digested this in silence. He had his breakfast quietly. He could not remember the last time when he had had breakfast in peace at home. He was usually constantly on his mobile phone, either talking to someone or checking his messages. He contemplated what he would do during the day. He had thought he would spend time with his wife, but she was not present at home. He had not asked her whether she would be available. He had assumed that she would be there for him.

After breakfast, he decided to watch television. He caught up with the news and flicked through the channels. He grew bored of watching the television after a couple of hours. He thought of reading. He looked through his collection of books and settled on a work of fiction. He read for an hour or so and then it was time for lunch. He had a quiet lunch and then decided to have a siesta. After his siesta, he did not know what to do. His family was still away from home. He enquired from his domestic help: 'At what time are they expected to be back?' But the help had no idea. So Verma went back to his book.

Finally, his wife came at 7 p.m., followed by his daughter and son.

'You are all late,' remarked Verma.

'Late?' questioned his wife, Anjali. 'But this is our normal time to return.'

'Normal?' queried Verma

'Of course,' replied Anjali. 'You have never been home, so how would you know?' she questioned.

'Where was Ria all this time?' questioned Verma about his daughter.

'She has coaching classes after college,' explained Anjali, 'and Ayush comes home by 7.30 p.m. or 8 p.m.'

Verma listened to her intently. He had always assumed his family returned home early. He had to put in long hours of work, and then socialize professionally. He realized he did not know much about what his other family members were doing.

They had dinner together after a very long time. Ayush was on the phone during dinner and spoke less and then excused himself after dinner. Verma was a bit displeased, but he kept his opinion to himself. His wife and daughter chatted about the day.

After dinner, Verma retired to his room. His wife was very tired and immediately fell asleep. He watched television for a while and soon decided to sleep as well. But sleep never came. He kept tossing and turning. Various thoughts crossed his mind. He finally fell asleep in the early hours of the morning. As a consequence, he woke up late, and again found the house empty. Verma just did not know what to do.

In this manner, a couple of weeks passed. Verma was at his wit's end. His life ahead seemed bleak. He had nothing to look forward to. He was a man who was not used to sharing his thoughts and feelings with his wife and could not bring himself to start now.

Verma had been a dedicated professional all his life. He had believed that his wife would look after his home and children. In the initial stages of his married life, his wife complained about his lack of time for her and threw tantrums. But Verma had simply ignored her.

Then came the children. First his son, and a few years later, his daughter. Anjali diverted her attention from her husband to the children, and looked after them. She was always there for them when they were sick or had problems. She attended parent-teacher meetings at school and made suitable excuses for her busy husband. Of course, she accompanied her husband to social functions—as was expected of her, but that was more out of compulsion than desire. She was the perfect wife.

They did not have too many conflicts. She was free to raise the children as she wanted to. He gave her money to spend and do whatever she liked. But the only thing he could not give her was time. She resigned herself to her fate and engaged herself with other activities. As the children grew up, she started writing. At first, there were a few articles which got published in some local newspapers. But she discovered that she had a flair for it and started writing fiction. Soon, she could get more of her work published.

Verma, at first, was surprised because he had not taken her writing seriously, but then he reconciled himself to the fact that his wife was a popular writer. He had thought it was a hobby to keep her preoccupied. But Anjali's popularity only grew. She was invited to literary discussions and talks in schools and colleges. She spoke well and soon became a much sought-after person at literary societies. So she was busy most days of the week, attending some event or another.

Verma had not really made any retirement plans as he thought he could not be replaced. He had always thought that he would be re-employed in a different capacity by the present government; therefore, he would be occupied for the next three years or so. He had never thought about what he would do after his retirement. Since he never shared any of his thoughts with his wife, she too never bothered to ask him anything. Now Verma really did not know what to do with his time.

Verma decided that he could look into his son's business and advise him, as he felt that he was an experienced person who had served in the government for so many years. But Ayush made it clear to his father that he could handle his own problems.

'But, beta, you can share your problems and plans with me,' pleaded Verma.

'You have never been there when I needed you,' replied

Ayush. 'Anyway, if I need to discuss anything, Mamma is always there,' he said in a matter-of-fact manner.

Verma could not believe his son had spoken to him in such a manner. He was very hurt.

Then again, one evening, he found his daughter coming home late and he questioned her. 'Why are you so late?'

Ria was surprised.

'Daddy, since when have you started keeping a tab on when I come and go?' she queried.

'It's not right that you keep such late hours,' replied Verma authoritatively.

'Daddy, I am coming back from the hospital as I kept my friend company. Her father had a nasty accident,' she explained.

Verma nodded.

Finally, Verma decided to speak to his wife. That night after dinner Verma told his wife about the two incidents. She listened quietly.

'Have you ever been there for us when we required your presence?' she asked softly. 'Yes, you have provided us with all material things. But does that count?'

Verma was quiet. That night he could not sleep. He had always put his career before his family. He always had important meetings to attend or important people to meet. He was so busy climbing the professional ladder of success that he had failed to see that he was neglecting his family.

The next few days, Verma was in a quiet and contemplative mood. The days were never-ending. He had nothing to do. He was depressed.

On some evenings, he had gone to the prestigious club—where he was a member—but he soon found out that the attitude of the people there had changed. The officers and businessmen who used to surround him, no longer sought his company now. He realized that they had hung around him only to access the power he had once wielded.

He spoke to a few retired colleagues and asked them how they spent their time. Most of them were happy indulging in hobbies, which they could not participate in during their service. One was playing golf, and others were writing, painting or making movies. Some were working for social causes and three others had joined political parties. Some of them were even busy looking after their grandchildren. Verma absorbed all this information.

What should he do? He had no hobbies. In fact, he realized that he had been obsessed with his career all these years. He did not play any sport or watch movies or go on vacations. He had been to several places in and outside the country, but those had been work-related tours. He really had no idea what to do and he was ashamed of asking for help. He was the all-powerful Verma. What would people say? He felt depressed. Even at home, he felt that he had no one to communicate with.

Then came the news that one of Anjali's new novels was going to be made into a movie. She was thrilled and so were the children. Verma felt a twinge of jealousy. The spotlight was going to be on his wife now. All along, he had been the important one in the family. He could not bear it.

The next few days were really difficult for Verma. He was saddened by his predicament. He knew he was being selfish and mean, but he could not help it.

But Anjali was astute enough to understand her husband's feelings, although he did not open up to her. She gently asked him what his plans were. She saw the bewilderment in her husband's face, and for the first time in her married life, she saw that he was unsure of himself.

Anjali told him that, first and foremost, he should look after his health. So it was best that he set up a routine for himself—maybe a walk in the morning. He could join a gym or learn a sport. He could even join an NGO, or even open an NGO to attend to a pressing social cause. He could teach children since he had had such a brilliant academic career. He could share his views on talk shows or in local television channels. There were so many options.

Verma was surprised by the number of options Anjali presented. He had never thought about it; he had been wallowing in his own self-pity. He saw his folly and how he had cut himself off from his family. He had taken them for granted. He would try to bridge the gap that he had created between himself and his children. Thank god his wife had not held it against him. She was such a confident and large-hearted person. He saw how he had narrowed his world.

'But not anymore,' he promised himself.

This would be a new beginning.

Religion

Nayan Sharma was the new rising star in Guwahati. His debut album was breaking all records. He had become an overnight singing sensation due to a melodious number on this maiden album. The song was on the lips of most youngsters. The soulful lyrics of the song and the romantic music ensured that the song became a chart-buster.

Nayan was elated. Success at the young age of twenty-one was something he had not dreamt of. He had started singing in school and continued to do so in college. He joined college competitions, sang at functions in his college and his neighbourhood. Music was his passion, but he had not known if it would ever be his livelihood. His mother had been a bit sceptical about his passion as she wanted him to earn a living with a decent job, but he was an average student. The only person who encouraged him to sing throughout the years had been his childhood sweetheart, Nasreen. She was the only one who believed in his abilities. She felt that he had a magical voice, which would mesmerize his listeners. She urged him to practice singing daily. When he started recording his maiden album, she went over the lyrics he had written and improved it with her suggestions. Nayan valued her opinion and feedback greatly.

Nasreen lived next door to Nayan. They had studied together since the first grade. In fact, both of them had been in and out of each other's homes since they were kids. Nasreen lived with her parents and elder brother. Both the families shared a good relationship. Nasreen considered Nayan's home to be her own. Their friends in school and college considered them to be best buddies and some even envied their closeness. Their friendship had deepened over the years and during their teens, they realized they were in love. It was something that everyone close to them had expected.

As she grew older, Nasreen grew closer to Nayan's mother. She would help her in her household chores and, at times, run errands when Nayan was unavailable. She was the daughter that Nayan's mother never had. Nayan also relied on her for every little thing. Nasreen's parents were broad-minded people. They trusted Nayan and treated him like a son.

After the album release, Nayan's popularity soared. Social media was a big boon for him. Thanks to it, people from all nooks and corners of the state now knew of him. He was very good-looking and the girls swooned over his looks and his voice. This was an unexpected bonus for him. He got a lot of offers to perform in stage shows. Seizing the opportunity, he, along with his band of musicians, started performing in functions. Slowly, the number of functions increased and the troupe began to be paid well.

Nasreen was happy for Nayan. True, now he was away from home a lot. But this was the time when he could build his career. He was beginning to get the recognition he had craved. He would have to work hard now and form his base.

He wanted to shine in his chosen field. He had found an opportunity and he would make the most of it.

The next few years were hectic for Nayan. He was creating new albums, singing at functions and was approached by several music directors to work for their projects. He sang in various languages and was invited to do shows in other parts of the country. He even started getting invited for shows with other popular singers abroad.

Throughout these years, Nasreen was always there for him. She looked after his mother and was always there for her as well. She would give her company when she was lonely or sick, accompany her to social events, take her for health check-ups to the doctor and assist her with any other thing she needed.

Nasreen had completed her education and was now employed in a school nearby. She did not earn very well, but since she loved children and teaching, she enjoyed her job. The mornings were very busy for her and she was very passionate about her work. She did miss spending time with Nayan, but she felt that he was working towards their future. She was proud of his achievements and wanted him to grow his career to the utmost limit.

Most of their school and college friends were either married or engaged to be married by now. Nasreen's family and friends were beginning to ask her as to when she would settle down. She just smiled and shook her head, but slowly, she too began to think about it. It was time for her to be married. She decided to ask Nayan about his thoughts during his next visit. He was away for long periods now, although he did call her every day.

So on his next visit home, Nasreen broached the subject.

Nayan listened to her and promised to speak to his mother immediately. Nasreen was happy that he too wanted to get married soon.

Over the next few days, Nasreen waited eagerly for the outcome. But Nayan seemed to be preoccupied with other things. He did not speak much. Nasreen was puzzled. Was something bothering him?

'Have you spoken to Ma?' asked Nasreen directly.

Startled, Nayan looked at her.

'I have to talk to you,' said Nayan quietly.

'About what?' asked Nasreen, bewildered.

'Ma is against our marriage,' he replied flatly.

'But why?' asked Nasreen, puzzled.

'Because we follow different religions,' he answered. 'She is worried about what society will say.'

Nasreen was stunned. She had never thought along those lines herself. Her parents had also never raised the issue. Because of her closeness to Nayan's mother, she had thought that she had been accepted. She had never imagined that Nayan's mother would reject her because of her religion. This was simply unbelievable.

The next few days were unbearable for Nasreen. She was in a state of shock. She could not believe that her dreams were crumbling. She had asked Nayan about his point of view. Nayan had evaded her eyes and responded that he could not go against the wishes of his mother. He was her only son and his mother had brought him through many hardships. He did not wish to give her any pain. He would agree to whatever his mother desired.

Nasreen's heart grew cold at this revelation. What about her? Didn't she mean anything to him? All these years that she had dedicated to his mother and him. Did they mean nothing to him? Had he even cared for her, she thought bitterly. She felt used. Nayan had not even fought for their love. He had just accepted his mother's view without even giving their love a chance. It was not their fault that they followed different religions. She could help them out with everything, but she was not thought suitable to be a part of their family because of her religion. She was heartbroken.

It was embarrassing for her to break the news to her family. Her brother was livid and wanted to confront Nayan, but she forbade him from doing so. The situation was difficult for both the families.

After a couple of months, Nasreen announced to her family that she had applied to a university in Delhi and wanted to do a course. She had been accepted and she would have to move to Delhi for a couple of years. Her parents readily agreed to send her away for higher studies. They were glad that she had taken control of her life despite being emotionally battered.

So, within a month, Nasreen headed for Delhi. The course filled her time and she made a lot of friends. She learnt new things and tried to forget her heartache. It was difficult, but she was determined not to wallow in self-pity.

After a few months, her brother informed her that Nayan's marriage had been fixed with a girl of his mother's choice. She hailed from Tezpur. This bit of news pierced Nasreen's heart. She was very disturbed for a few days. All her rosy dreams had crashed. She tried to block out the happy memories of her times with Nayan. She had not kept in touch with him after his decision to not marry her. Their mutual friends had been shocked and there had been a lot of gossip amidst their social circle. Nasreen had borne the brunt stoically. She did not blame Nayan and refused to give people any fuel for discussion.

On completion of her course, Nasreen headed back to her home. She was lucky to get another job in a different school. So she joined work immediately and became busy.

On the third day, when she was coming back from school, she saw Nayan's mother in her veranda. She tried to greet her, but the old lady avoided her and went inside. Nasreen shrugged and went home. Over the next few days, she saw the old lady several times. She would often be peeping from the window or waiting in the veranda. The old lady avoided eye contact with her, and if Nasreen happened to look her way, she would turn her face away.

Nasreen told her mother about this peculiar behaviour of the old lady. Then her mother told her that Nayan's wife did not look after his mother. Nayan was now based in Mumbai. His wife had prevailed on him to settle there as it would provide him with better opportunities to grow his career. Nayan had left for Mumbai and his wife had stayed back. His wife did not get along with his mother. As the days passed, their differences grew. She filled Nayan's ears with complaints against his mother. Nayan finally decided that he would take his wife away from his mother, to Mumbai, with him.

At first, Nayan visited his mother as often as he could. But slowly, his visits became few and far between. His mother yearned for company, but she knew her son was slowly, but surely, drawing away from her. She could simply do nothing to bridge the gap.

Nasreen absorbed this information. She was a soft-hearted girl and her heart went out to the old woman. She was astounded by Nayan's behaviour. Had she loved such a shallow man? The man who had forsaken his love for his mother's wishes was now behaving so callously with his mother. How was this possible? Had his celebrity status changed him so much?

One day, when Nasreen was coming back from school, Nayan's mother called out to her. Surprised, Nasreen walked towards the old lady.

'I am sorry for all the pain I have caused you,' the old lady apologized.

Nasreen was taken aback. She opened her mouth to speak.

'No, let me speak first,' said the old lady. 'I have not been able to face you after the wrong I have done. I have committed a big mistake and done you a great injustice. I did not appreciate your sweet and kind nature. I was only bothered about what society would say. Is society bothered now?' she questioned. 'Religion doesn't matter at all,' reflected the old lady.

'Can you do me one last favour?' she finally asked.

'What, aunty?' questioned Nasreen.

'Can you find me an old age home? I am growing old and frail. My health is deteriorating every day. I will not be able to continue with my daily household chores,' she explained.

'I have no other option than to stay in an old age home,' she concluded with, tears rolling down her eyes.

'What about Nayan? Doesn't he look after you?' questioned Nasreen in distress.

'He hardly visits nowadays,' she stated. 'Neither does he call or send me any money. I have been living on my meagre pension,' revealed the old lady.

Nasreen was shocked at the revelation.

'He has no dearth of money,' she thought. 'Why has he changed so much?'

'Call him once in my presence,' said Nasreen.

The old lady took out her cell phone and called him twice. The dial tone ended. He had not received his mother's call. Nasreen understood the situation. She knew what she had to do.

She looked for the best old age home. She settled Nayan's mother there and promised to visit her from time to time.

The old lady did not know, but Nasreen had paid for all her expenses.

Remorse

It was a cold December morning, but Usha was sweating. She was in labour and the pain was becoming unbearable. It had been a good twelve hours since she started labour. It was her first time. She was in a small village, near Tirap in Arunachal Pradesh. The village was located in a remote area. There were no medical facilities available. A midwife was attending to her.

Usha had no other option.

She was the leader of an insurgent group in Northeast India. She was in the core group and was a dedicated member. Inspired by her brother who led the group, she had joined the group at the age of nineteen. She had already devoted ten years of her life to the cause, which was freedom of her state from India. There were few other women in the group. It was a hard life as they were on the move quite frequently. The camps were located deep inside jungles, in areas inaccessible by roads.

The chairman of the organization had decided that the women members should get married. While some of the women chose their own partners, it was Usha's brother who decided that she would marry the commander-in-chief of their army. Usha had no objection, and the commander-in-chief agreed as well. So, they were declared man and wife. Now, a year after their marriage, Usha was about to give birth. The only problem was the fear of getting caught by security forces. So she had been placed in a remote village with no medical facilities. Her husband could not accompany her. She knew that this was the safest thing to do and so, she was accompanied by two other females cadres. Together, they traversed from their camp in the Myanmar-Arunachal border and came to this remote village after walking many miles, a couple of days ago.

After three more hours of painful labour, a son was born. Usha was elated but exhausted. Of course, the moment her son was born she forgot all her pain. She decided to name the son Surya.

Usha knew that she would need some time to recuperate. So it was decided that she would spend at least a fortnight in the village. She knew that it was risky to stay for such a long time, but she had no option.

It was on the seventh night after the baby's birth that the security forces found her. They had surrounded the village with a huge contingent. Usha knew she could do nothing. She had been captured. Someone from the village must have leaked information to the forces. She was a big catch, after all. She was a high-level leader involved in the decision-making processes of the organization.

Usha was taken to her state—Assam. The operation had been a joint one, conducted by the police forces of Arunachal Pradesh and Assam. The information had been received by the Assam Police and so she was shifted to Margherita Police Station.

At first, Usha was in a state of shock. The father of the baby had not yet seen the child. She did not even know whether he was aware that she had given birth. When would he know? When would he see the child? What would happen to her and the child now? These and thousand other questions plagued her.

Usha and her child were first taken for a medical check-up, as was the norm. Usha was found to be healthy, but her child was developing jaundice. This information worried Usha. She had not dealt with children before, much less new-born babies. The attending doctor asked her if the baby had been given any vaccinations. She replied in the negative.

She and the baby were produced in court. The courtroom was packed as people were aware of her arrest and had come to catch a glimpse of her. The judge put her in custody with the police for ten days as they wanted to interrogate her.

Usha was taken to the police station.

She was interrogated by the station house officer and a female deputy superintendent of police. She decided to keep mum. At first, the interrogators were patient with her. But after an hour passed, and Usha kept her lips sealed, the interrogators started to lose their patience.

Her baby awoke and started crying. She fed him, but he was still crying. Bewildered, she did not know what to do. Meanwhile, the superintendent observed that something was wrong. She tried to pacify the baby.

The doctor was called. After examining the baby, he suggested that the baby should be shifted to the nearest hospital in Digboi, a few kilometres away.

The police immediately arranged for the baby to be shifted there as the Digboi hospital was better equipped and also had a child specialist in attendance. The next two days were agonizing for the mother. The baby was kept in the intensive care unit as his bilirubin had increased and had high fever. Usha was only allowed inside the intensive care unit to feed the baby. She had never felt so alone and helpless. The only thing that she could do was pray.

After three days, the baby's health started to improve. Usha knew that her baby would never have survived had she been in the village. She was thankful that she had been captured. The security forces had acted promptly and provided the baby good medical attention, which would otherwise have been impossible for her to access.

Usha and her baby were taken back to Margherita after a five-day hospital stay. The police decided to start the interrogation immediately as they had lost precious time. She was taken back to the interrogation room and questioned. This time, she answered questions in monosyllables and ensured that the police would learn nothing from her.

The police grew frustrated. It was soon evening and another day had been lost. The nurse came in to see the baby at the centre as it was difficult for the police to take them every time. As per the doctor's advice, the baby had to be vaccinated. As the nurse took out the injection and made preparations, Usha winced. How much pain would the baby have to suffer?

The interrogators saw the mother wincing, and immediately, the lady officer addressed her, 'Usha, you are wincing when your baby is being vaccinated?'

'Yes, madam,' replied Usha. 'Look at his size! He has been through so much in the past week and now this injection will hurt him,' she said, cringing at the thought.

Immediately, the officer answered, 'You do not want to see your son in pain. But have you ever thought of all the mothers who have lost their sons because of the senseless killings by your organization? The injection is just a prick for your son and it is for his own good. But think of all the irreparable loss which you have caused for all mothers,' she said harshly.

Usha fell silent at this unexpected verbal onslaught. She had never thought about the mothers, the families or their feelings when it came to the people who had been killed by their organization. They were doing it for a cause, for the motherland. She had never thought about it emotionally.

That night, she could not sleep. She kept tossing and turning in her bed. The harsh words of the officer rang in her ears. But wasn't the officer right? What about all the mothers who had lost their children because of their organization's beliefs? How devastated they must have felt. She could not even bear the thought of her son being sick! How could she have turned off her emotions while carrying out missions for her land? Wasn't she behaving mechanically? What had come over her? Was working for the organization ever the correct decision? Had she been swept away by the fiery speeches made by the leaders? She did not know what was right and what was wrong.

She was tormented by feelings of guilt and her lack of conscience.

As morning dawned, she came to a decision. She would leave the organization. Her new-found conscience was not allowing her to continue. She could not be responsible for more killings. She would cooperate with the security agencies. Her son would not have survived without the prompt action of the security forces. He had received excellent medical aid, the kind which was beyond her own means. She wanted her son to grow up in a free world, without fear, unlike what her life had been for the past eleven years.

She was tired of being constantly on the run from security forces. No, her son would be like the sun she had named him after. He would be strong and free.

Retribution

The grand wedding was finally over. Swati was exhausted after the rituals. It had been a long day for her. It was time for her to bid farewell to her family. She had been dreading this moment. How would she leave her near and dear ones to live with complete strangers? Unlike other brides, she was not looking forward to this. She was just twenty-one and had completed her graduation. She wanted to do her Masters. She had dreams for herself. But all her dreams had been shattered a few months ago.

Her father had come back from work one evening, very excited. A respectable family had sent a proposal for marriage through a relative. They wanted Swati for their son, Yash. Yash was four years older than Swati and would make a good match. He was a businessman, as was his father, and helped with the family business. He had a younger sister who had been married off a few months earlier. Swati's mother was ecstatic. Swati had two younger sisters. So like typical Indian parents, her parents too always worried about the future of the girls.

Swati understood her parents' predicament. But she still hoped she could follow her dreams. But this was not to be.

Her family made enquiries about the family and came to the conclusion that there could be no better match for their daughter. They asked a relative about the expected dowry. The reply received was that there were no demands for dowry, as the family understood that Swati's family, the Kaushiks, would do what's best for their daughter. Mr Kaushik could not believe his luck. Dowry was a major source of worry in their community. He had been worrying about it ever since the birth of his daughters. The pity of his friends and relatives had increased his apprehensions.

But god seemed to have heard his prayers. A respectable family and a well-educated son-in-law. He had been saving for the marriage since Swati's birth. He vowed to spend to the extreme and celebrate the wedding with pomp and splendour. And though there were no demands from the bridegroom or his family, he ensured that he would give them befitting gifts. After all, it was all for his eldest daughter, the apple of his eye.

And so, Swati stepped into her new home to start her married life. The Bharadwajes were very happy with their new daughter-in-law. The gifts that they had received were more than their expectations. Swati was a beautiful girl and matched their handsome son, Yash, perfectly.

Meanwhile, Swati, too, had adjusted to the fact that she could not pursue her studies. When she met Yash, she was swept of her feet. He was very good-looking and she was attracted to him instantly. Her friends and family kept reiterating the fact that she was a really lucky girl to be marrying into such a respectable family.

So, Swati started her married life with new dreams. Immediately after her marriage, they went on a honeymoon to the Maldives. This was a dream come true for Swati. The beautiful island and her handsome husband ensured that her honeymoon was perfect. The expenses had been paid by Swati's parents, but she was not aware of it.

After the honeymoon, Swati tried to adjust to her new home. It did not take her much time to understand the routine of the household. She also understood that her mother-in-law had the final say around the house. Yash was an obedient son and consulted his parents on most matters. He worked hard on his family's business and went to work early. Her father-in-law also worked there, but at a more relaxed pace. He was teaching Yash the tricks of the trade and was preparing him to take over the business entirely.

Meanwhile, Swati, too, was trying to familiarize herself with the house. She was very hopeful that her in-laws would allow her to continue with her studies. The topic was raised through Yash, but the idea was immediately struck down by her mother-in-law.

'Why should Swati study? We are there to look after her needs,' said Mrs Bharadwaj to Yash.

Yash could not argue with his mother. He conveyed the news to Swati with a heavy heart.

For Swati, this came as a bolt from the blue. Until then, everything had been perfect. Swati's parents had told her that she could pursue her studies after her marriage as her in-laws had assured them about it. But she realized that it was not to be so. Swati was upset. However, she took it in her stride and reconciled herself to the fact that she would not be able to continue with her studies.

The next two months passed uneventfully. Then one day, her sister-in-law, Nisha, called. It was a short and tense phone call. Swati did not understand the cause of this agitation. She did not try to pry into their affairs. When Yash came back from work, he was immediately summoned by his parents. The three of them had some discussion in her in-laws' bedroom. Swati continued with her household chores. She was curious, but she did not ask any questions. Yash would tell her in good time.

The atmosphere in the house was tense for a few days. Yash remained tight-lipped. Swati was hurt. She felt like an outsider. She knew something was wrong, but she had not been included in any of the discussions.

She finally questioned Yash about it. But he was unwilling to tell her anything. In fact, he pretended that it was all in her imagination. Everything was all right. Swati was astounded by this denial. She decided to keep quiet about it.

Slowly, everything in the household changed. Her mother-in-law started finding faults in her regarding simple things. When Swati protested, she was scolded. Her mother-in-law even complained to her father-in-law about her. She was called rude, arrogant and argumentative. Swati was shocked by the turn of events. She was sure that Yash would understand her. But when she tried to explain her version of events, Yash would hear none of it. He asked her to mend her ways and listen to her mother-in-law.

Swati was bewildered. Everything had been perfect the first couple of months. Yash had been a perfect husband and his family had treated her like a daughter. But she did not understand why or how things had changed so suddenly.

She decided to keep herself busy, and to keep her point of view to herself. Whenever her parents called her, she was careful not to speak about her woes. She painted a rosy picture of her married life. She did not want to be a cause of worry for her parents.

For the next few days, it seemed like the household was attaining normalcy. Swati went out for a movie and dinner with her husband one weekend. It seemed just like her honeymoon days. Her husband was attentive and loving, just like he had been in those days. Swati came back from the dinner in a happy frame of mind.

But when they came back home, Yash was again summoned by her in-laws. He came back to sleep late but Swati was awake. Yash seemed thoughtful and preoccupied.

Swati prayed for normalcy to return within the household.

The next morning, as was her habit by now, Swati was up early. After her daily prayers, she started her chores in the kitchen. Her in-laws were usually early risers. But that day, they got up late. They seemed to be in a bad mood. Her mother-in-law came to the kitchen and started finding faults in Swati's work. Her father-in-law also found faults with the breakfast she had served. Yash gave her disapproving looks. Even though the whole household seemed to be against her, Swati kept her cool.

Over the next few days, Swati tried to keep out of her in-laws' way. She was tired of her mother-in-law's taunts and accusations. She refused to rise to her bait. Her father-in-law was rough and rude to her. She wondered what the problem with the family was, but could not fathom an answer.

Tired of the negative atmosphere, she spoke to Yash, asking if she could visit her parents. Yash spoke to his mother and Swati was allowed to visit her parents for a week. This came as a relief to Swati. She could not wait to go back and left for her home eagerly. At least she would be able to stay with her parents and siblings in a loving environment for a few days.

Swati's family was happy to have her for a week. Her parents pampered her and her sisters updated her about everything that had happened after her marriage. Swati decided to keep her troubles to herself. She did not want to worry her family unnecessarily. She went out with her friends, watched movies, ate at her favourite restaurant and enjoyed herself. But she did not forget to make a daily phone call to her mother-in-law, enquiring after the well-being of her family.

All too soon, the week had passed. Swati wished she could prolong the visit, but she knew that was not possible. Being a practical girl, she observed that at least she had had a refreshing break from the oppressive atmosphere at home. She would try to be positive. With such thoughts, Swati went back home.

But the situation seemed to have deteriorated. As soon as she stepped into the household, Swati knew that something was wrong. She held her silence and did not ask any questions.

Yash told her the problem at night. Due to some bad decisions, the family business had suffered some serious losses. He did not tell her while she had been at home as they did not want to disturb her during the break. They were trying to find ways and means to minimize the losses, but had not been successful.

Swati took in the news. She knew her husband was a hardworking man. The family business had been doing well for so many years now. This came as a huge shock. She hoped that her father-in-law, who had many years of experience in the field, would come up with a solution.

A few days passed in a tense atmosphere.

Yash was always away having discussions with his parents

at night. Swati did not ask any questions. Yash would tell her if there was any positive news.

Then one morning, Swati's mother-in-law started her taunts again. For the first time, her mother-in-law started insinuating that Swati had not brought any dowry. As they were from a respectable family, they had not demanded any. But Swati's parents should have understood.

'Don't they want to see you happy?' asked Mrs Bharadwaj. 'After all, they would be giving it to their daughter, not someone else.'

Swati was dumbstruck. She had not in her wildest dreams thought that her mother-in-law would be speaking about dowry.

Swati was very disturbed. That night, she broached the subject to Yash. Yash heard her out and slowly replied that he agreed with his parents.

Swati was speechless. She could not believe her ears. Her well-educated, suave businessman husband had expected a dowry! For a few seconds, she could not breathe. She felt choked with different emotions. The man whom she thought she could rely on was now singing a different tune. She thought she had been married into a respectable, progressive family. But all that had been an illusion!

Swati's nightmare had just begun. Slowly, her in-laws became more vocal about the dowry. They asked her to call her father and ask for money. At first, Swati refused and their taunts fell on deaf ears. She did not want to burden her father as she knew he had done his best. He had spent a lot and had a grand wedding, gifting her in-laws and husband with lavish gifts. He had two more daughters to think of. How could she ask her father for money?

Then, slowly, the mental abuse turned physical. The first time she was physically abused was when Yash slapped her as she adamantly said that she would not call her father for money.

'Why can't you understand that we need to gather money to save our business?' shouted Yash.

Swati was thunderstruck. She had never been slapped or beaten at home, even when she was a child. She had only heard about such horrific acts. And now it was happening to her. She could not believe it. Tears streamed down her face.

That night, she could not sleep.

The next day, Yash apologized for slapping her. He was full of remorse. Swati was a soft-hearted girl and she forgave her husband immediately. And after that, for a few days, things were better between the couple.

However, the abuse started at the behest of her mother-in-law. Her mother-in-law asked Swati to hand over her jewellery. Swati refused. Yash beat her up for this and Swati was then compelled to hand over her jewellery.

'Once our problems are over, you will get back your jewellery,' promised Yash.

But Swati knew that this was a false promise, just like the other promises that he had broken. Her handsome husband listened to his parents and did not care about his wife. He was too weak to take her side.

A few days later, Swati realized she was pregnant. She should have been elated, but all she felt was a sense of helplessness. She did not break the news to her husband or her in-laws. For the time being, she decided to keep it a secret.

Swati had lost weight due to the constant mental torture she was going through. She worked hard and was constantly on her feet as well. She had become pale and her skin lacked lustre. Her unhappiness could be seen clearly on her face. Nevertheless, she did not let her parents know about her predicament.

One morning, there was another short phone call from her sister-in-law, Nisha. Swati's mother-in-law was highly agitated after the call. Yash was called in from work and they had a discussion behind closed doors. Swati wondered what the problem was, but she was never allowed inside the room during these discussions. She could not ask the house helps about it either as they had been working for the family for a long time.

Swati pondered about the call. She realized that from the very first day she had never been accepted into the household. She had been treated like an outsider. Her husband would be called into her in-laws' bedroom whenever there was anything important to be discussed. She could never go in, and she could never be part of the family in the real sense. She was tired of having to live with such tension every day and the torture was getting to her. She bore bruises on her face and her body and even her mother-in-law had started hitting her. She had nowhere to go. She had not even completed her studies. She would not be able to fend for herself if she left her husband. She could not go home to her parents. Her family would be shunned by the society and marriage prospects for her sisters would be ruined. She was in a catch-22 situation. There was no respite for her.

One night as Swati finished her chores after dinner and was heading towards her bedroom, she heard her mother-in-law speaking from the behind the closed bedroom door.

'We will have to do away with her, Yash,' she said. 'She is too stubborn and we need the money.'

Swati stood rooted to the spot. They were talking about killing her. She could not believe that they would go to such an extent for their greed. She came to her senses and quietly moved away. She was not safe in this house. She had to act fast and immediately.

Swati headed to her room and gathered the small amount of money she had. She changed her clothes and fled the house at night before her husband could come back to the room to sleep. In her panic, Swati had left with no idea about where she was going. She hailed an auto and headed for the bus terminal.

Luckily, she was in time to catch a night bus to her hometown and she left Jaipur for Lucknow. Once the bus left Jaipur, Swati started to breathe easily.

She had had a lucky escape. God was with her. She had no option but to return home now. She was never going to come back to her in-laws. If her parents did not want her, she would go elsewhere. She would find a job, any job, even cooking and cleaning would be fine, but she was determined to not go back to her husband.

'How spineless could my husband be?' she fumed. She only felt contempt for him now.

Her troubled thoughts kept her awake for most part of her journey. She fell into a dreamless sleep towards daybreak and she reached Lucknow early the next morning.

Her family was surprised to see her. She broke down and told them all about her ordeal. They were horrified by the tortures that she had been through. Her mother held her and wept; her father also had tears streaming down his eyes.

'Why didn't you tell me?' he asked her. 'How could you go through this alone? Didn't you have any faith in us?'

Swati was relieved after she had shared her ordeal with them. She decided to take a bath and sleep.

'We have to let your in-laws know that you are here,' said her father.

'Do we have to?' implored Swati.

'Yes, we do,' he replied. 'But don't worry. You will never have to go back to that house,' he swore.

Swati took a bath and came out for breakfast. Her parents were waiting for her. She looked at her father's face and knew that he had some news.

'What is it?' she asked.

'I called Yash to let him know you are safe,' said her father.

Swati nodded. 'And…?'

'Nisha, your sister-in-law, has been burnt by her in-laws for dowry,' replied her father.

'What!' exclaimed Swati, astounded.

'Yes. Apparently, she was being harassed for her dowry,' replied her father.

Things fell into place for Swati. Nisha was being harassed to pay a dowry. To meet that demand, they had harassed their daughter-in-law, Swati. Yash had been a pawn in the game. The Bhardwajes had lost both their daughters and their unborn grandchild.

Swati realized she had a providential escape.

Sacrifice

The alarm sounded with a shrill ring. Havildar Harish Rai woke up at the sound. It was still dark outside. He had set the alarm for 4.15 a.m. Since it was winter, he did not want to leave the cozy blanket at once, so he gave himself a minute or two. He slowly rose for his morning ablutions. He usually woke up before the alarm could ring. Years of practice had done that for him and his body got used to rising early. But last night, he had slept much later than his usual bedtime.

His days always began very early. He had to be on the training ground before 5 a.m. and he always reached the ground at 4.55 a.m. Twenty-eight years ago, when he had joined the Assam Police Force, he had woken up at 4 a.m. every morning for his training. He had continued the habit even after he passed training which turned out to be good for him.

He had been posted in the training institution for the last twenty-five years. And in the police training institutions, work began early every morning.

He was a trainer and he took his job very seriously. He

had been a good trainee when he had been inducted into the service and had won all the awards. He had been sent for higher training to other places in India and had excelled at them all. So it came as no surprise to him when he was posted in the training institution as a trainer. It was his job to mould the 'new boys' and train them to his satisfaction. He knew that the quality of the personnel in the force depended on the trainer.

He was a dedicated person and he expected his trainees to give their 100 per cent on the training field. He knew most of the trainees were in awe of him. The manner in which he handled weapons inspired the new boys. He could open and assemble weapons in seconds, even blindfolded. His style of teaching was different from the other instructors and the trainees instantly connected with him and were eager to learn from him. They aspired to be like him.

Harish Rai knew he was a role model for his young trainees. He tried to live up to their expectations. He did not drink or smoke, lest his trainees picked up these bad habits from him. The other instructors cribbed about being posted in the training institute. They would rather be out in the field. But for Harish Rai, it was a matter of pride. He was an easy-going person who was happy with what life had to offer him.

Two years after he had joined the service, he got married and was eventually blessed with two sons. His family life was blissful and he could devote time to his wife and children, unlike other policemen. And he knew that this was possible because he was posted in the training institute; if he had been posted in the field, like his counterparts, he would have had very little time to spend with his family. Now, as a trainer, he could give his family ample time. He felt he had the best of both worlds—professional as well as personal.

The sixty-third batch of sub-inspector trainees were currently training at the training institution. Havildar Rai had been entrusted with the task of training them along with some of his colleagues. The trainees were an intelligent lot. They were freshly out of college and the training period for them seemed to be an extension of their college life. Although Havildar Rai was strict, he enjoyed teaching them. He always loved imparting guidance to the fresh trainees rather than instructing trainees in refresher courses. The ones who came for refresher courses had already been in service, and they usually went through the course because it was compulsory. On the other hand, fresh trainees were full of enthusiasm with a drive to learn something new each day. This enthusiasm was loved by the trainers because it gave them a boost while training.

This particular batch was now in their ninth month of training. There were quite a few pranksters in this batch and some of their pranks were rib-tickling. But, of course, the instructors could not appear to be tickled by it. They had to maintain a facade. Havildar Rai himself had a couple of favourites: Sandeep Haloi and Deepjyoti Nath. Both trainees were great friends, but tried to outdo each other when it came to their pranks. But it was all harmless fun and, therefore, everyone enjoyed their antics. Despite fooling around whenever the opportunity arose, both the boys were quick learners. They picked things up fast and even helped the slower ones in the batch to bring them to par with the group. This trait endeared them to their batchmates.

Rai observed that in every group some trainees were quick learners and others took their time. Often, there was a lot of rivalry among the trainees. He encouraged healthy competition amongst them because it egged them on to perform better. Competitions helped sharpen the skill of the trainees and bring out the best in them. So Rai used this to the best of his ability.

It was a Friday. Rai was going to teach his class about grenades. He planned to show them a live grenade, so that his trainees got the general idea. It was a theory class and his trainees would get a glimpse of a grenade. This would prepare them for their practical classes. For the practical class, they would be taken to the firing range. The firing range had small hillocks. The practice was to take the trainees up the hillock in small batches and from there they would throw the grenades down the slopes. That way, there was little chance of any accident taking place. The trainees were given grenades only during the final boards. So each trainee got one chance to throw a grenade.

Rai began class in his customary way. He realized that the whole class was listening to him with rapt attention. He explained the science behind the grenade. Then he showed them the 36-high explosive hand grenade. He showed the class the percussion cap, the time delay fuse and the lever. He gave them the specifications and observed the boys furiously noting down the information. After forty-five minutes, the whistle blew, indicating the fifteen-minute break. Usually, the boys would wait eagerly for the break. But today, since the grenade was a fascinating topic for the boys, they took some time to filter out of the class.

Rai carefully kept the live grenade on a table along with other items. He had already instructed the trainees about the perils of handling a grenade. He then went out to join his fellow instructors for a short tea break. His throat was parched after having spoken continuously for forty-five minutes, answering the queries of the trainees.

Exactly at 4 p.m., the whistle blew for the last class of the day. Some of the trainees were already in the classroom, waiting for the instructors to resume the class. Rai strode across the corridor and entered the class but the scene that met him chilled his heart.

The whole class was sitting, waiting for his arrival, but his two favourite trainees were playing with the hand grenade. He made a roar of anger at their foolhardiness, despite his repeated warnings during the previous class. His arrival and his roar of anger took the two boys, Sanjay and Deepjyoti, by surprise. Startled, Sanjay who was holding the grenade dropped it to the ground. The lever was still left in his hand.

Rai took in the situation and made a split-second decision. He pushed the boys out and the other trainees made a mad scramble towards the exit. Rai flattened himself over the grenade with a dive to take the impact. A couple of seconds later, there was a loud blast and his body was blown into smithereens. There was a splintering sound and window glasses shattered.

A few trainees sustained minor injuries, but the only casualty was Havildar Rai.

He was cremated by the side of the lake. A stone was erected in his memory. But there was no epitaph. No words could convey the deep emotions of the trainees, his colleagues or the superiors.

His sacrifice had been supreme.

Second Chance

Dr Abhijeet and his wife, Dr Antara Goswami, anxiously waited in front of the emergency department of the hospital. They had brought their eighteen-year-old son, Aveek, to the hospital a few minutes ago. He had consumed pesticide and they had found him unconscious in his room. They were horrified that their only son had tried to commit suicide. They swung into action and saw that he was barely alive. They immediately brought him to the hospital, but they were not allowed into the emergency room.

Abhijeet and Antara were in a state of shock and disbelief. Their son had tried to take his life. But why? They could not understand it. They were perplexed. He had always been a good and obedient boy. In fact, they had not had much trouble while raising him. He was a good student and a very talented musician. He sang very well and played the guitar. He loved music and had a lot of friends. He seemed like such a happy child. They could not fathom the reason behind taking such a step.

They both started praying to the Almighty. Antara was crying; Abhijeet was lost in his thoughts. This was a nightmare.

Where had they gone wrong? Why had he taken such a step? There were so many questions racing through their minds. Had they been too busy for their son? They did not seem to have understood him or his needs. They hoped fervently that they had brought their child to the hospital at the right time.

His pulse had been low. Had they been a little late, he would have passed away at home.

The next hour felt like eternity for the couple. The wait was killing them. There was no news from inside the department. Both of them kept looking at the door anxiously. Abhijeet paced down the corridor and Antara wept quietly. Finally, the doctors came out.

Aveek was out of danger, but he was very weak. The parents silently thanked god. Aveek was allotted a room and would have to stay in the hospital.

Aveek studied at a reputed school in the city. His father was a reputed surgeon and his mother was a gynaecologist. Both of them were extremely successful in their profession. Aveek lived in a beautiful home and had been brought up by a nanny. Their home was looked after by a housekeeper and there was a vehicle kept aside for Aveek, with a driver who drove him to school. His parents ensured that Aveek had the very best of everything, be it school or anything else that he desired.

Aveek was a level-headed boy. He was an obedient child who loved his parents. Although his parents had very little time for him, he understood the importance of their job. Theirs was a happy family.

At a very young age, Aveek discovered that his interest was music. He loved to sing, and indulging his interest, his parents enrolled him for music classes as an extracurricular activity. Aveek was a keen learner. He sang very well and also learnt to play the guitar. His parents were proud of his musical skills. However, he did not neglect his studies. His parents had instilled in him the importance of a good education, and Aveek had always been a good student. During his teens, he started taking part in music competitions and would always win a prize.

With some of his friends, Aveek formed a band. They practiced regularly and started performing on stage. At first, they played in their school. But slowly, their reputation grew. They were invited to perform at festivals and events. Aveek loved to perform on stage and their performance was always well appreciated by the audience.

Aveek knew how to balance his studies and his music. His parents were proud of him. He passed his tenth board examinations with flying colours. It was after his tenth year that Aveek's problems began. He wanted to study humanities, but his parents wanted him to study science. He was good in all subjects, but he wanted to study English, and finally pursue music. But his parents did not let him have the chance to voice his opinions on the matter. They had already decided that he would study science.

So Aveek reluctantly joined the science stream. The coursework was vast. It left him with very little time to pursue his extracurricular activities. Aveek was enrolled in science tutorial classes. So, apart from the time he spent at school, he had to attend his tutorial classes. He also had a lot of assignments and had to work hard. He could not manage to fit his music classes into his schedule, but he did manage an hour sometimes to listen to music.

His parents wanted him to study medicine after school.

Aveek was, however, averse to the idea. The very sight of blood repulsed him. He knew, in his heart of hearts, that he was not cut out to be a doctor. He told his parents about his feelings but they were adamant. They opined that every student felt like he did in the beginning, but once they started attending classes, these feelings disappeared.

The next two years were tough for Aveek. He studied hard but was miserable as he could not practice or learn music. He did not want to disappoint his parents, so he worked hard. He was pulled between his desire to please his parents and his desire to follow his passion, which was music. His close friends knew about his turmoil and they urged him to speak to his parents.

Aveek tried to speak to his parents many times. But whenever the topic arose, they would brush it aside. He felt trapped. He even went to the psychologist at his school and opened up about his feelings, where he was again advised to speak to his parents.

Aveek finally decided to speak to his parents after he sat for his twelfth board examinations.

◆

Aveek answered his twelfth boards and then sat for the entrance examinations for medical and engineering colleges. He also applied to Delhi University because he wished to study there. He was a good student and he passed his twelfth board examinations with a good percentage. He was waiting for his NEET (medical entrance) results. A part of him wished that he would not qualify for the course, but the good student in him wanted to know how he had fared in the exam. Many others in his place would have purposely done badly to disqualify for the course. But Aveek was not a boy who could deceive his parents. He prided himself on being a good student.

Aveek's parents walked into the cabin. Their son was asleep, saline was being administered to him. He looked pale and weak. His mother sat down beside him. He would take time to recover. Why had he decided to end his life? It was still a mystery to them. Or was it?

Antara started to think. Abhijeet interrupted her thoughts.

'Let me go home and bring his essentials since he has to stay the night,' said Abhijeet.

Antara nodded tiredly.

After his departure, Antara started thinking again. Aveek had been a happy child with many friends. They had been a close-knit family. He would apprise them of all that was happening in his life during school. She was aware of his likes and dislikes. She knew about his friends, teachers, fights, competitions and every aspect of his life. She prided herself about being a mother who was very close to her child. Aveek also knew he could confide in his mother. She was always there for him, as was his father.

Where and how did this change?

She thought hard. In his teenage years, Aveek became a bit reserved. Antara was apprehensive. She kept a close watch on her son as there were many stories of children going astray during their teens. She decided to keep vigil. There were many students his age who tried smoking, drinking and even drugs. But after sometime, Antara realized that Aveek did not indulge in these vices. Nor was her son crazy about the opposite sex like some of his schoolmates. He had simply become reserved in a mature manner. He had his share of fun in harmless ways; his one constant passion was music.

He did not miss a single day of practice.

Antara was satisfied with her son. He was growing to be a good and responsible boy.

Then Antara and Abhijeet joined a new and upcoming hospital. Their workload had increased as their time at home decreased. Sometimes, they had to go to the hospital at odd hours. The earlier, fixed hours of working had now changed. Their salaries had, of course, increased a lot. But the change had meant less time to spend with the family.

They wanted their son to become a doctor, just like them. So from a young age, they impressed on Aveek the need to study hard and do well. To them, no other profession was better than medicine. Both Abhijeet and Antara's fathers were doctors and so they wanted their son to continue the legacy.

Aveek had first voiced his opinion when he was in the eighth standard. During a family gathering, some relatives had questioned Aveek about what he would like to become when he grew up.

'A musician,' Aveek had replied immediately, without hesitation.

Abhijeet and Antara had been taken aback. The next few days, they impressed on Aveek the wonders of the medical profession. They also pointed out that unless one had loads of talent, it would be impossible to make a decent living as a musician. Aveek silently listened to them. They thought that they had made their point. The matter was not discussed again.

After his tenth board examination results, Aveek told his parents that he would like to study humanities. This caused an uproar in the family. There was emotional blackmailing. So much so that finally, Aveek had to take up science as his stream. His parents were relieved. He tried to tell his parents that the sight of blood made him nauseous. But they laughed at him and tried to pacify him by saying it happened to all first-timers.

Aveek had not known how to get his point across. Finally, he had decided to go along with the flow.

Antara and Abhijeet believed Aveek had gotten over his fears and aversion to medicine. Last week, the NEET results were declared. Aveek had qualified for medicine. He had gotten a seat in his hometown to the delight of his parents.

◆

Abhijeet came into the cabin with Aveek's belongings. He was holding a single sheet of paper.

'What is it?' asked Antara.

'Read it,' said Abhijeet curtly.

Antara took the piece of paper and read it.

'Dear Mummy and Papa,

I cannot do it. I will never be able to fulfil your dreams of becoming a doctor. My passion is music and you will always be ashamed of me. I am ending my life as I could not be a worthy son.

Love,
Aveek

P.S. I love you both.'

Antara's hands shook and tears streamed down her eyes. Her face was ashen. She looked at her husband.

'We have failed him,' she cried. 'He has always been a good son. We tried to foist our desires and ambitions on our son.'

Abhijeet hugged her.

'Yes, we are failures as parents,' he replied. 'We never understood him or tried to understand his passion or love. We are to blame for his drastic step.'

Aveek opened his eyes slowly upon hearing all the noise.

'Mummy, Papa,' he spoke weakly.

'Yes son,' they spoke in unison, rushing to his bedside.

'We are sorry,' apologized Abhijeet.

'We did not try to understand you,' said Antara.

'No more,' swore Abhijeet. 'You have been a good son. From now onwards you will follow your dreams'

'Really, Papa?' questioned Aveek.

'We promise,' said Antara.

The three of them held each other. God had been kind. They had nearly lost their son. They were given a second chance.

The Betrayal

'All is fair in love and war,' thought Amrit, as he and Deepa were pronounced man and wife after the long rituals. He looked at Deepa's beautiful face and thought, 'Yes, I have done the right thing.'

He was satisfied. After many years of first setting eyes on Deepa, she was finally his. He still could not believe that she had agreed to their marriage. He thanked god that he finally got what he had wished for.

Amrit and Deepak had been friends since kindergarten. They had studied in the same school, lived in the same neighbourhood and their parents were family friends. They went on to study engineering at a prestigious college in Delhi together.

But this is where the similarity ended. Deepak was always the brilliant one, faring extremely well in academics. He was a good sportsman as well. Amrit, on the other hand, was definitely much better than the average student, but could not match up to Deepak in either academics or extracurricular activities. Deepak was also the better looking of the two. So it was no wonder that Deepak got more attention from the girls.

They were in their third year of engineering when both of them set their eyes on Deepa. She was a fresher and her striking beauty caught their attention almost immediately. Both of them vied for her attention and were attracted to her simple yet charming nature. But Deepa did not pay attention to either of them. She was a studious girl, friendly, but not aware of her charms.

But slowly, over a few months, as she settled into the college, she made a lot of new friends. Deepak and Amrit were amongst her new friends. Deepak, as was his nature, was out to win her affections. They found that both of them had a lot of common interests. Deepa was, of course, bowled over by Deepak. And it was evident to all their friends. Soon, both of them became inseparable.

Amrit had, in his heart of hearts, always accepted that Deepak had better qualities than him. But somehow, he could not accept the fact that Deepa had preferred Deepak over him. He watched their growing friendship from the periphery. At times, he cursed himself for not expressing his feelings for Deepa in time. Maybe, just maybe, Deepa would have reciprocated his feelings then. At times like these, he felt his resentment against Deepak growing. Although, outwardly he was friendly with both of them and did not display his feelings, inwardly he was consumed with a feeling akin to hatred towards Deepak. But since they had been childhood friends and he could not do anything about his feelings, he continued his daily routine.

Two years flew by and it was time for graduation. A lot of their friends had been selected for jobs in prestigious companies, while some others decided to pursue higher studies. Deepak had decided to pursue higher studies and had applied to a few universities in America. With his brilliant academic career, he was selected into a prestigious university. Amrit, on the other hand, decided to join his family business as it had always been expected of him. And he had not thought differently.

Six months after graduation, Deepak went to America for higher studies and Amrit joined his family business. It was hard for Deepa to see Deepak go. They had almost been inseparable during the past year and she knew that it was for their future that Deepak was trying so hard to excel. Deepa too planned to follow Deepak to America. She studied hard, determined to follow his footsteps. She missed him terribly, but she was a sensible girl and tried to immerse herself in academics.

Amrit was glad that Deepak had moved to America. The last year had been unbearable for him. He had had to pretend to be happy for his friend and Deepa, whereas, the relationship was totally unacceptable to him. He wanted Deepa's love and he would do anything to obtain it. Thoughts of Deepa and how to win her love consumed Amrit's thoughts.

After a lot of thought, he came up with a devious plan. He was in touch with Deepak regularly and also met Deepa every other day. Slowly, innocently, he started dropping hints to the other that they had started developing separate interests. He sowed seeds of doubt in both their minds. He would do it so innocuously that neither suspected him of lying.

Of course, both Deepak and Deepa were in touch regularly, talking through WhatsApp calls and video chats. But, at times, certain things Amrit had said could not be verified, as Deepa was busy with academic pressure, projects and deadlines, and Deepak too was settling down at his university, trying to keep up and adjusting to the new environment. So Amrit's insinuations affected them slowly, and doubt began to creep in. After a month or so, when both Deepak and Deepa started confronting each other with alleged happenings, the situation worsened. The distance was a great barrier as many things could not be talked about. There was frustration and unhappiness in store for both Deepak and Deepa. Eventually, things came to such a state that they ended the relationship.

This was the opportunity that Amrit was looking for. He did not lose any time and took full advantage. Deepa was at an emotional low, and she obviously turned to Amrit for solace. Meanwhile, there was a crisis at Amrit's house. Cancer had been detected in his father's liver and doctors predicted that he had very little time. Amrit and his family were heartbroken.

Amrit wanted to make sure that the remaining days of his father's life were as comfortable and happy as he could make it. Amrit's father wanted to see his son settle down. He had already taken over the reins of the family business and his father wanted to see him get married.

Things moved so quickly that Amrit did not know what to do. Deepa was still in her third year of college. But when he told his family about Deepa, they met with her parents and told them of their predicament. Deepa's parents had no objection to their marriage, and because of the extraordinary circumstances, agreed to solemnize the marriage at a very short notice.

So within a month, in spite of Deepa still being in college, they were married. Although the circumstances were not how this marriage was envisaged by Amrit, he was only too willing to have his dream come true. He was secretly gloating about how easily he had manipulated events to his advantage.

The only glitch was his father's health.

And so began Amrit's married life. Deepa continued to attend college and Amrit slowly immersed himself in the nitty gritty of business affairs. After a month or so, Deepa complained of fatigue and weakness. Amrit, as a concerned husband, took her to the doctor without much delay. To his happiness, he found that Deepa was pregnant. He was ecstatic. His happiness knew no bounds. His family, too, were overjoyed at the unexpected turn of events. Only Deepa seemed to be drawn and listless. Amrit thought that this was because of the timing, since Deepa was still in college and it complicated things for her.

Amrit took good care of his wife. His father also seemed to be doing a little better. It seemed as though he was willing himself to live to see the birth of his first grandchild. Only Deepa seemed to have moved into a deep shell. She was polite but reserved and seemed to be lost in her thoughts most of the time. Amrit tried everything to cheer her up.

After five and a half months, one night, Amrit was woken up by Deepa. She seemed to be in labour. Amrit rushed her to the hospital. He was not prepared for such a turn of events as there were a few months to go before she was to give birth.

Deepa gave birth to a healthy baby boy after being in labour for ten hours or so. Amrit's joy knew no bounds. He rushed to thank the doctor. The doctor congratulated Amrit. Amrit voiced his concerns to the doctor as the baby was premature. The doctor assured him that the baby was perfectly healthy as it been in the womb for a full term.

Amrit was shocked. How could that be? It had not even been six months since his marriage. He decided to confront

Deepa at once. Deepa was tired after the long labour and seemed even more listless. When Amrit confronted her, she was quiet. Then, looking directly into Amrit's eyes, she boldly told him that the baby had never been his. It was Deepak's.

The announcement shattered Amrit. He could not believe it. Had he been cheated? But was he? Hadn't he cheated his childhood friend and robbed him of his happiness? Destiny had played a cruel game. He could not tell anyone. He would have to live with this lie all his life! Who had, in reality, cheated whom?

The Change

Priya had just turned forty, but no one who saw her would have said so. She looked so much older—a good fifteen years older. She had gained a lot of weight and her long tresses were turning grey. She was developing wrinkles.

She had two children, aged nineteen and sixteen. Her husband looked much younger than her.

She had been married for twenty years now. It seemed like yesterday when Arjun had come to 'see' her. She was a beautiful, lively girl, enjoying her college life. She had not wanted to get married and be tied down to domesticity, but meeting Arjun had changed her mind. Arjun was very good-looking and courteous, and he had swept her off her feet.

Looking back, she did not know how twenty years had passed. After marriage, she had lived with her in-laws as Arjun was the only son. Her in-laws were loving and she got on well with them. A year after her marriage, she gave birth to a girl, and a couple of years later, a son. For the next few years, she was busy looking after her children and the home.

Meanwhile, Arjun worked in a multinational company, and had started concentrating on his career. He had no worries as far as the house was concerned. He had a lovely wife who looked after his children and home very well. She was efficient and they shared a loving relationship. His wife gave him all the space that he needed and he respected her for that.

On the day of her fortieth birthday, Priya had gone to the nearby supermarket to buy some groceries. She ran into one of her school friends, Sheila. They had met after a gap of almost fifteen years and it took Sheila some time to recognize Priya.

'My god, Priya! Is that really you?' exclaimed Sheila. 'I wouldn't have recognized you if you hadn't called out to me!'

'Have I changed so much?' asked Priya self-consciously.

'Of course, you have,' exclaimed Sheila. 'Where is the pretty, stylish girl that we all knew?'

Priya was startled. She chatted with Sheila for some time, exchanged phone numbers and came home.

On returning home, Priya had a good look at herself in the mirror. A middle-aged, overweight woman looked back at her. She was dressed in a saree, with vermillion on her forehead, her hair tied in a bun. This was in direct contrast to Sheila who looked so young and was dressed in a pair of jeans and a top.

But was it because of her attire?

'No,' thought Priya, 'it isn't my attire.' Somehow, it was her entire personality that made her youthful. Sheila was slim and moved around confidently, which was natural as she was a successful entrepreneur. Priya thought for some time, but she could not pinpoint the reason as to why she looked so different.

In the evening, after finishing her chores for the day, Priya sat down to make her customary phone call to her mother. She saw that her number had been added to a new

WhatsApp group. Curious to find out who had added her, she checked and found out that Sheila had added her to her school friends' group. She was overjoyed.

She immediately started texting and connecting with all her old friends: Runa, Neera, Asha, Mayuri and Ritu. They, too, started communicating with her. She was kept busy the whole evening, chatting with them. She did not know how the time flew by.

Arjun came in late and she quickly served him dinner. He was tired and went off to sleep. Priya continued to chat with her friends till late in the night. She came to know about their present whereabouts, what each one of them was doing and what each one looked like at present. Everyone started posting pictures of themselves and their families. Two of her friends were unmarried. They were married to their professions, they joked.

Priya became a bit self-conscious when it was her turn to post a photograph. Compared to her friends, she looked old and seemed to belong to a different age group altogether. As she went to bed that night, she thought about all her conversations with them. Her friends seemed to be doing so many interesting things. They seemed to be—what was the word her children used?—Yes, they were 'chill'. She really felt like a middle-aged aunt compared to them. That night, sleep eluded her.

She was up early the next morning. She went about her morning chores in a thoughtful mood. Mid-morning, she sat down for a much-needed coffee break. She reflected on her life.

Was she unhappy? Not really. She had been too busy looking after her family. Theirs was a happy household and she had been instrumental in making everyone happy. Then why did she have the niggling feeling that something was not right?

That night, she confided in Arjun. She told him about her meeting with Sheila and her WhatsApp group. She went on and on about her friends and her feelings, when she suddenly noticed that Arjun was fast asleep. She sighed. No one seemed to have time for her. Arjun was always home late. He was almost always too tired for any conversation. On weekends, they would meet their relatives and friends or go for a movie. Her children were also busy. When they weren't at school or college, they had their guitar or tennis lessons or birthday parties to attend.

All this while, she had never noticed it. She had been too busy cooking, cleaning or shopping for household goods. Then she had made time for her in-laws too. They were growing old and she looked after them well.

Somewhere along the way, she had had no time for herself. Yes!

She realized what the niggling feeling of doubt was.

When was the last time she did anything for herself? She even wore the clothes Arjun had bought. Did she ever listen to a song she liked, or watched a TV series she enjoyed, or read a book that she wanted to? She had buried all her desires and wishes in order to keep her family happy. When and how had this happened? She was bewildered as the realization dawned on her.

She was being taken for granted by her family. Did she want to continue in this manner? She was troubled. The world seemed to have progressed, but she seemed to have been stuck in a time warp. Even her family, whom she had given twenty years of her life, had no time for her.

As she thought, she kept reading the WhatsApp messages in her group. Even her friends who were housewives like her had interesting lives. She did not have any topic to converse with them—apart from her family and movies. At least many of her friends had kept in touch with each other. Some had joined the gym, others met for coffee or occasional movies. She realized that she did not have any real friends after her marriage, only acquaintances in the form of her husband's friends' wives or interaction with mothers of her children's classmates.

She introspected the whole day. Her family did not notice her self-absorption. She continued with her chores and nothing seemed amiss to them. She pondered over her problem and tried to find solutions.

Meanwhile, in her WhatsApp group, her friends were planning to have a reunion. It had been ages since they had met. Priya, too, wanted to go. But did she want to go like this? Yes, on the surface everything was fine. She had a perfect family and every member of her family was doing well. But what about herself? No, she had to do something about herself.

She thought about it the whole night. What changes did she want in herself? Physical change? Yes, 100 per cent. She felt unfit. She didn't want to be a size zero. But she wanted to make herself more presentable. What about her soul? She needed to feel at peace with herself. She would find time for herself every day. What was it called? Yes, 'me time'. That was absolutely necessary. She would have to adjust her daily routine a bit. She didn't want to upset her family. It was not their fault that she made no time for herself. She did not want them to suffer for her inadequacies.

The next day, she went about her plan. She enrolled herself

in a yoga class nearby. Every evening, she would attend yoga classes. She was free early in the evenings as her husband and children came home only by 7.30 p.m. or so. She also resolved to wake up an hour earlier than usual and go for long walks in the neighbourhood. That would take care of her physical activities.

She had also wanted to learn to play an instrument in her younger days. She wanted to learn the violin. On enquiring about it, she found out that there was a music school nearby. She was self-conscious at first, as she thought that she must be the oldest student there, but on joining the classes, which were held in the afternoon, she found a friendly bunch of people attending with her. As she interacted with other students, she started feeling at ease. She enjoyed learning.

After a few days, Priya, who had been a good painter, decided to start painting again. After finishing her lunch, instead of her usual siesta, she set up her canvas and opened the bottled colours of paint. She stared at the blank canvas and the palette of colours in front of her. She was filled with a sudden eagerness and took the brush. She became so engrossed in painting that she did not know how the next couple of hours had passed. She was reluctant to put down the brush.

Priya felt the release of some emotion she could not identify. It was only because it was time for her yoga classes that she had stopped painting for the day.

Meanwhile, her family had no inkling about this change in her. The only fact that they noticed was that Priya had taken to going for morning walks regularly. They did not know that she had found a new meaning to life.

Priya made new friends at her yoga and violin classes. She even got to meet many of her neighbours during her morning walks. Although it was difficult for her in the beginning, she slowly started enjoying her morning walks, and soon found it invigorating. It also became the time when she felt the peace and quiet of a new day and made her daily plans.

A good two months later, her family noticed the physical changes in her. She had lost a lot of weight and her skin was beginning to glow.

Priya decided to have a makeover. She cut her long tresses into a more manageable hairstyle, taking away years from her face. She changed her style of dressing. She loved experimenting and shopping for herself now.

Her husband was astounded. The children were speechless. Priya herself seemed so much more confident.

They brought up the topic at the dining table. But Priya had only one answer to their queries; she said it was something she owed to herself and it was long overdue. Her husband looked at her with new eyes.

Then, her family learnt about her painting.

'But they are beautiful, Ma,' exclaimed her daughter.

Her husband agreed, taking a long look at the paintings. Priya smiled at their reaction.

'Why don't you sell them, Ma?' questioned her son.

'I am just painting for my inner satisfaction,' replied Priya. 'The paintings are not good enough to be sold.'

'Maybe we can frame them and put it up in the living room?' suggested her husband.

Priya nodded her assent.

Her husband made a mental note that he would seek an opinion about selling them. His wife was talented.

The Homecoming

Meera was excited. She was coming home after fifteen years. She had boarded a flight for the first time. She had only seen aeroplanes on television before. But she was glad that she was not alone. Her employer, Riya Didi, was accompanying her. There were so many procedures to go through at the airport. She would not have been able to get through all of it alone. Riya Didi was used to travelling. Meera just had to follow her.

Now, here she was, inside the aircraft.

Meera was apprehensive, but the aircraft took off smoothly. She was travelling from Mumbai to Assam. It would be a three-and-a-half-hour journey. She looked around to see what her fellow travellers were doing. Some were reading, others were working on their laptops, and others were taking a nap. Riya Didi was working on her laptop.

Meera decided to relax. The morning had been hectic for her. Getting up early, travelling to the airport and checking in. Now that she was finally travelling home, the memories started pouring in. Memories of her childhood and her home.

The first few years of her life had been happy for Meera. She lived with her parents in a small village named Ahata

Guri Gaon, near Tezpur town in Assam. She had two brothers and two sisters. Her parents worked in agricultural fields. They were very poor and their parents had to work very hard to make ends meet. She remembered leading a carefree life in the village and playing with other children, but she could not recall their names. She had attended school, but she could not remember anything that she had been taught there.

And then, one day, she heard her parents discussing an uncle who had come to visit the village frequently. The uncle lived in a big city, outside Assam. He provided young children with employment as he had a lot of contacts in the city. Many families in the city were composed of working couples who needed help with household chores and someone to look after the children. These couples often preferred young girls from a village and the salary was good.

The uncle had come over to their house and made the same proposition to her parents. He could arrange employment for Meera. She was only twelve at that time. Her sisters were aged five and three. The parents considered the proposition. Times were hard for them. It was becoming increasingly difficult to feed their huge family of seven. Sending Meera to work would mean extra money and also a mouth less to feed. There was nothing to lose. So after a long discussion, they decided to send Meera to the city for employment.

Meera was happy to know that she would be going to the city as this meant that she did not have to go to school. She had been hit with a cane quite often by the school teacher and she was not very fond of learning her lessons. She only went to school because she was compelled to. So this was an easy way out. Moreover, she would be going away from her village to the city. She would have different experiences, see different sights.

She was happy to know that two more girls from her village would be accompanying her. She was excited at the prospect of leaving her village and going out to the world as very few girls had been out of the village.

So after a couple of days, early in the morning, Meera bid goodbye to her family. Her mother packed her clothes in a small bag and made her some pitha to eat on the way. She felt important as everyone bade her tearful goodbyes. Uncle promised to bring her home every year. Satisfied that they had taken a good decision, the parents saw her off.

The journey had been a long one. She remembered travelling to Guwahati on a bus. The journey had taken four hours. Green fields, trees, houses and small village hamlets sped by. One of the other girls was sick on the bus, but Meera sat near the window and stared at the changing scenery. They reached Guwahati by noon and she was amazed by the noise and bustle. So many vehicles and the huge buildings! They had had a meal at a small hotel and then proceeded to the railway station. The three girls were excited at the prospect of travelling on a train.

They boarded the train in the evening. It was a long journey and it took them four days to reach Mumbai. The three girls loved the journey as they soaked in new sights and ate different types of food. They were surprised by the variety of food, the different types of people and the bunk beds on the train. After reaching Mumbai, they lodged in a small and dingy hotel. Mumbai was crowded and noisy. But they were too exhausted from their long journey when they reached their hotel at night. After dinner, they lay down exhausted in their beds for a good night's rest.

The next morning, after a bath and fresh change of clothes,

the uncle took them in an auto to an area called Kamathipura. The auto navigated through dingy lanes and finally, deposited them in a ramshackle building with dirty stairs. The girls were taken and made to sit in a room while their uncle went inside. After a while, he came out with a middle-aged lady wearing a bright saree. The lady examined the three girls and decided that she would keep Meera. They haggled over prices and money was exchanged.

Uncle told her that she would have to work for the lady and bade her goodbye.

Meera was terrified at being left alone, but the lady held her firmly. Meera did not like the lady and she did not like her new environment. She found that there were older girls in the house as well. Excluding her, there were six other girls. She was shown her room, a small dingy space where she deposited her belongings and looked around. There was a small window with grills and a bed in the room. She would be sharing her room with another girl.

She was then taken through the house, which had small rooms and common toilets. The dining area was bigger and there was also an attached kitchen.

Meera was wondering about the nature of her chores. Would she have to work in the kitchen? The other girls were introduced to her. Then, an older girl named Rakhee was asked to show Meera her work. The other girls were curious about her and asked Meera about her home and family.

'What kind of work do I have to do?' asked Meera innocently.

The other girls looked at each other.

Only in the evening did Meera learn about the type of job she was supposed to do. Having no inkling about it, she was horrified. She protested and cried, but to no avail. She was initiated into the oldest profession.

She could not believe that the man her family had trusted had sold her into a brothel. She felt cheated and tainted. The emotions she felt could not be explained. She was angry at her destiny. She felt helpless and trapped. She was disgusted.

It took her a long time to reconcile herself with her fate.

The years rolled by, and each day was more or less the same. New girls came into the house and reminded Meera of the first time when she had entered. It was a prison. There was no escape.

At times, she fell ill and was looked after by the other girls. She, too, looked after them if they fell ill. The girls considered each other as family. They sought solace and comfort in each other. Sometimes, Meera wondered about her own family. Did they think about her? Did they miss her? Did they ask the uncle about her? What lies had he fed her family? Would they ever try to seek her out? Did they receive any money for her services? Or had they forgotten her very existence?

With the passage of time, her memories of her childhood faded a little. She could not remember the names of all her childhood friends, but the memory of her parents and siblings were etched in her heart. Would she ever see them again?

Then, one night after thirteen years, there was a police raid in the area. The girls were rounded up and taken to the police station, along with the lady who Meera worked for. Meera was bewildered. There were cameras and media people everywhere; the police personnel treated them roughly. They were herded into waiting police vehicles. There was a huge commotion in the area and the girls huddled together, seeking comfort in each other.

The next morning, they were produced in the court and then sent to an NGO. The NGO staff were kind and treated them compassionately. They were housed in a women's home. The home was big, nice and airy, unlike the dingy small rooms they were used to. It was in the NGO that Meera first met Riya Didi.

Riya Didi owned the NGO. The NGO asked the girls their particulars, their names, parents' names, and addresses. Some of them could give the authorities their addresses, while others had forgotten. Many of them had come to Mumbai at a tender age. Meera gave them her parents' names and the name of her village. She told them she was from Assam.

The NGO tried to trace the family of the girls.

Among the many, two of them could be sent home after a couple of weeks. The family of two other girls did not want them back and the girls were heartbroken at the news. The families of three other girls could not be traced. Meera's information was inadequate. Meera was full of hope that she would be reunited with her family soon. But the NGO could not trace her village, as the information provided by Meera was sketchy.

The NGO enrolled them in various classes to provide them with vocational training. Meera wholeheartedly tried to learn. She knew that she had to learn some skills to be eligible for employment. She was illiterate and had to survive. She was a smart girl and so she learned quickly. She was soon lucky to be employed in a leather factory, which made bags. She was thankful that she could earn her living legitimately.

Meera, along with the other girls, started living in a rented accommodation near her work place. They had to move out of the women's home as it was a temporary solution, but she never forgot Riya Didi and kept in contact with her regularly.

After two years, Riya Didi gave her good news. Riya had been to a meeting in Delhi, where she had met people working in an NGO in Assam. Riya had provided them with the details and description of Meera's village and asked them to help her trace Meera's family. The NGO had called Riya and informed her that there was a village of the same name near the small town of Tezpur. Meera's family had been traced!

And so, Meera was homeward bound with Riya Didi to help her. Meera was excited at the prospect of meeting her family.

After landing in Guwahati, they checked into a hotel for the night. Riya Didi hired a vehicle for their journey to Tezpur the next day. Early the next morning, they proceeded to Tezpur. It took them three and a half hours to reach there. In Tezpur, they met the members of the NGO from Assam. One of them offered to take them to Meera's village.

It was a forty-five-minute ride. Meera looked around with interest. The roads had been widened, but the paddy fields were just like how she remembered them, green and bright. A few new buildings had come up, like houses and schools. Finally, the vehicle stopped in front of her house in the village. A number of kids came to inspect the car and the occupants.

Meera was excited and her heart beat loudly. She was apprehensive too. Would her family remember her?

A man came out of the house, followed by a woman, and they both looked at Meera questioningly.

Riya asked them about Meera's father's whereabouts. The man replied that he had passed away five years ago.

Meera took a moment to absorb the news.

Then the man introduced himself as the son.

Meera looked at her brother.

'Do you recognize me?' she asked hesitatingly.

The man shook his head.

'Meera,' she introduced herself.

Recognition dawned on the man. Another man and woman came out of the house.

'This is Meera,' said the first man.

Everyone stared at her.

'Where is Ma?' she asked.

'Ma has also passed away,' replied the man.

Meera's legs felt unsteady.

'We know where you were and what you have been doing all these years,' said her brother. 'Uncle was arrested a few years ago. He told the police that he has sold many girls to brothels in Mumbai.'

'So, they knew where I had been sold,' thought Meera.

'There is no place for you in this home. For us, you never even existed. Please go back and never come here again,' said her brother in a loud and clear voice.

Meera was thunderstruck. The harsh words pierced her heart. Her dreams of a family reunion were shattered forever. This was her reality; she had no family. The family she had pined for had never really cared for her. She was only the money-making machine.

She turned away, blinded by her tears. Riya Didi stretched out her hand to support her.

The ride back to Guwahati was made in silence. The verdant green fields, the clear blue skies, she would think about them no more. As the car picked up speed, she stuck her head out of the window, taking in one last long look.

She took a deep breath before erasing it from her memory forever.

The Lost Child

The year was 1996. Shibu Murmu had gone to the nearby town of Kokrajhar from his village, Lungsung. He had some work to do in the office of the deputy commissioner of Kokrajhar. He had to apply for a ration card. His family was large; he had three children, two sons and a daughter. The sons were named Jitu and Raju, aged ten and eight, respectively. His daughter, Malati, was five and was the apple of his eye. His aged parents also lived with him.

It took Shibu a good two hours to finish work that day, but he would have to come again next week. He decided to drink some tea in a shop near the deputy commissioner's office before heading back home. He met a couple of acquaintances there and was just sipping his tea when suddenly, there was a commotion near the tea stall. Shibu looked up and saw a couple of men shouting.

An extremist organization had attacked a village and several people had been killed.

With the cup of tea still in his hands, Shibu went closer to the group of men who were talking. Apparently, the attack had taken place during the afternoon and several villagers had been killed.

'Which village, brother?' Shibu asked one of the men.

'An Adivasi village,' replied the man. 'Lungsung.'

Shibu stood still for a moment. He was shocked.

Then his heart started to hammer loudly and the blood rushed to his head. He felt dizzy.

'What's wrong, brother?' asked the man.

'It's my village,' replied Shibu in a whisper.

Then he controlled himself. He had to rush to his village and find out what had happened. He threw his cup of tea and started for home.

When he reached his village, he saw the place swarming with army and police forces. He heard wailing and cries of distress. He made his way towards his house, anxiety writ large upon his face. The sight that met his eyes confirmed his worst fears. The militants had killed his parents. He saw his wife, Gita, wailing loudly, and his two sons in shock, sitting hunched beside her.

'Gita,' called Shibu, reaching out to his wife.

Gita looked at him with blank eyes at first, then comprehension dawned on her.

She started blabbering. A group of militants had entered the village and started shooting at the villagers indiscriminately after lining them up. Around twenty villagers had been killed. Shibu's parents, who were inside the house, were dragged outside and killed. Even young children were not spared. The youngest casualty was a two-year-old. They had killed her ruthlessly.

Gita had been working in the paddy fields. The fields were situated at the outskirts of the village. Their fields were even further away, near the hills, and were therefore saved.

They had heard the gunshots from the fields and hurried

home to find the villagers killed.

'Malati?' questioned Shibu, his heart turning cold.

'I left her with your parents,' replied Gita. 'But now I cannot find her.'

Shibu's heart skipped a beat. He started to sweat.

'Let me go and check the bodies,' he said quietly.

Shibu went ahead and started checking. His neighbours, friends, and so many others had been killed, but there were only three children among the dead. Where was his daughter?

Maybe she was afraid and in hiding. He started to search for her. His sons followed suit. They combed through the entire village but could not find her.

Shibu then reported the matter to the police. He was asked to file an FIR. He had no other option. He was grief-stricken. He had lost his parents and did not know the whereabouts of his daughter.

Two days passed in a flurry of activities. He had so much to do. After the formalities ended, he had to perform the last rites of his parents. There was no time to mourn the loss of his parents, as he had to search for his daughter. The whole family started searching for her, but to no avail.

The Adivasis had lived peacefully for years in this village. They were on good terms with the Bodo villages nearby. Then why had this happened? It was true that the Bodos were agitated and afraid of becoming a minority in their own land. They feared that the Adivasis were out to grab their land and livelihood, but that was no reason to attack them, and unprovoked. Shibu could not comprehend the gory killings. Why? For what purpose?

Thoughts of his precious daughter consumed him day and night. Where was she? How was she? How could she have simply disappeared? She must be missing him. She must be frightened and lonely.

The villagers who had survived the massacre were shifted to a relief camp, and many other villages were evacuated. Shibu systematically started searching through all the camps. He went to the police station every day in the hope of getting some information, but his search was not fruitful.

Days passed and months rolled by. Life in the relief camp was not easy. The number of inmates began to rise as the ethnic clashes increased. This posed a greater problem to the inmates. Shibu survived through these difficult times with his family, but a void remained in his heart when he thought of his daughter. He continued to be hopeful and looked for her even after the other members of his family and friends gave up.

The situation slowly improved between the two communities, and finally, after a year and a half, Shibu could go back to his village with his family. The process of building their lives again in the village consumed his time. He toiled relentlessly, as did his wife; they had a bit of help from his sons now. Nearly three years passed in such a manner.

Shibu was in a better state financially, but he still grieved his daughter. His wife was racked with pangs of guilt. She had been inconsolable initially. Slowly, however, she had accepted the loss. Deep within themselves, they still hoped to find their daughter someday.

Then, one day, in the winter, Shibu happened to go to the market to sell his agricultural produce, accompanied by his wife. The market was filled with people. By afternoon they had sold more than half his produce.

He was resting and idly looking at the throng of people, when he saw her. Malati. She was taller now and dressed in a dokhona (the traditional attire of the Bodos). She was holding the hands of a Bodo woman.

Shibu gazed at her, shocked. Then he gathered his wits and slowly drew his wife's attention to her. His wife gave out a small cry of surprise. Instantly, they rose in unison and rushed towards their child. The mother could not help but hug Malati and shower her with kisses. The child gave a startled cry. The woman who had been holding on to the child cried out in alarm.

There was a small commotion and a lot of curious bystanders gathered.

'She is my daughter,' claimed Gita.

Shibu nodded his head. The child looked bewildered.

'Can't you recognize your mother and father?' questioned Gita.

Malati took a step backward, uncertain, and spoke to the lady accompanying her in Bodo.

'What is she saying?' questioned Gita.

'She says she doesn't know you,' replied one of the bystanders.

Gita was distressed. Gita and Shibu started speaking to her in their language, but the child just stared back, unable to comprehend what they were saying.

Eventually, Shibu asked the lady where she had found the child.

The lady replied that the child was her daughter.

By now, the crowd around them had increased. As a result of the commotion, the policemen on duty had also come over.

Unable to come to a solution, as both the parties claimed the child was theirs, the policeman took them to the police station. There, the officer-in-charge knew Shibu because of his constant visits. Shibu told him that this was his missing child. The Bodo woman also said that the child was hers. The impasse continued for some time. The officer-in-charge said that he would make enquiries in the village. The Bodo lady's husband came to the police station after some time had passed.

The husband then revealed that they had found the child five years ago, near Lungsung village, with a stray bullet injury on her leg. She was bleeding profusely and was unconscious, near a road. They had taken the child home and treated her wounds. The village medicine man had also treated her injury and it had taken the child some time to recover.

The husband had enquired at the neighbouring villages, but he could not find her parents. He had not gone to Lungsung village as the villagers had left the village for the relief camp.

The child did not speak much at first. The Bodo couple were childless and believed that this child was god's gift to them. They pampered her and smothered her with love. So much so that the child forgot her own birth family and her traumatic experience. She started regarding the Bodo family as her own, and she slowly forgot the Adivasi language. She picked up the Bodo language and adjusted to her new surroundings.

The officer-in-charge asked her if she recognized Shibu and Gita? Everyone waited with bated breath. The child slowly shook her head, answering in the negative. The officer-in-charge asked her whom she would like to live with.

The child pointed to the Bodo family.

Shibu and Gita were horrified. Their own child had not recognized them and was now refusing to come back to them. What was wrong with her? Where had they gone wrong?

The Bodo lady was apprehensive. God had answered her prayers for a child five years ago. Would the child now be taken away from her bosom? She silently prayed to the Almighty as her world now revolved around the child. She looked at her husband for support.

Shibu looked at the officer-in-charge imploringly. The officer-in-charge looked at Shibu and shook his head. He could not force the child to go with Shibu and Gita. The stark reality struck Shibu. His daughter, whom he had been pining, for five long years, was alive and well.

He had found his daughter, but he would never be her father again.

The Offer

Saurav Sen was resting in his room. He was awaiting the results of his test. Unlike the others, he did not feel anxious. He had been feeling unwell over the past few days. At first, he had thought that it was the seasonal change in weather that had affected his health. He had a runny nose and a dry cough. Five days passed, and then he developed a fever. He had been going about work despite feeling slightly unwell. It was not his nature to take rest. He liked to keep himself occupied at all times. He was not the kind of man to sit and brood. There was so much he had to do. There was so much he could do. Work had always been his priority.

Saurav Sen was seventy years old. He was a bachelor. His love had turned sour and had made him cynical about the institution of marriage. The girl he loved and wanted to marry had betrayed his trust at a very young age. He had been very angry and felt humiliated when she had spurned him. Since then, his feelings about love and marriage had undergone a drastic change.

To keep himself busy, he had joined a political party. His friends had urged him to join the party to distract his attention from his failed love story. He initially joined the party as a worker. Gradually, as he started attending meetings and rallies, he was drawn towards the ideology of the party. He could identify with its beliefs. He started going through the literature of the party. Reading through the reams of paper and the books widened his knowledge about the party—their history, their manifesto, elections, goals and beliefs. Slowly, he immersed himself in the work and became a dedicated party worker.

He wanted to work for the upliftment of society. He wanted to improve the state of affairs in his home state and country. He did not want to be a famous leader. All he wanted was to work for the betterment of society.

His family was surprised by his decision of joining a political party. He had never shown any interest in politics. He had always been an extrovert and was interested in sports. They did not know that he had been jilted by a girl. His two siblings were much older than him and he was the pampered youngest child of the family. He was reasonably good at his studies and his parents had many expectations from him. They had thought that he would study further, try for a good job and lead a comfortable life. They could not fathom how or why he had chosen politics, as the family had no interest in it either. They only mandatorily voted during elections. But they did not try to reason with their son as they believed in his ability to make his own decisions. They did not dissuade him.

However, they were worried about his livelihood. It was all very well to be immersed in politics, but how long would his siblings support him after his parents had passed away? They had their own families to look after. They tried to discuss the matter with Saurav, but he was not bothered.

Finally, his father decided to open a restaurant for him, so that he could have something to fall back on.

Saurav was happy with the arrangement. He did not have too many needs. As he dove deeper and deeper into the activities of the party, his personal needs lessened. He spent time at his restaurant in the beginning, but he was lucky as his restaurant did not require much time from him. This enabled him to spare most of his time for his passion—politics.

At first, he worked on the lower rungs of the party. He attended all the meetings and absorbed all information. He tried to propagate the ideologies of his party amongst his friends and relatives and even succeeded in recruiting others into the party. Gradually, as the years passed, the leaders of the party noticed his dedication. They knew he could be relied upon and he was given more responsibilities.

As for his family, they resigned themselves to the fact that he would not marry. Rather, he seemed to be married to the party! Slowly, they adjusted to his odd timings. They understood that his life and interests were different from theirs. He was there for his family when they needed him. He would help his friends and family. He was very reliable. He would be there to lend a helping hand in any crisis or celebration, but after that, he would go back to his work at the party.

Saurav's position in his party was good. His opinions were valued by the leaders. He was consulted on important matters. He was a good organizer and this fact was noticed by the seniors and leaders. In the beginning, he was asked to organize small events, but his skills were so apparent that the seniors asked him to organize big events. And so, he organized for the party in his city and brought discipline to it.

When he was in his forties, both his parents passed away

due to an illness within a short duration of each other. Saurav had looked after his parents in their last days. He was grief-stricken for a few days, but life had to go on, and he picked up from where he had left off. Now he immersed himself into his work at the party more than before.

In this manner, three decades passed. Saurav had become a senior member of the party and was given additional responsibilities. It was then that catastrophe struck the world. The Covid-19 pandemic started in China and spread to the rest of the world. The virus reached India too. There was a lockdown in the country. Many people were afflicted with the disease and hospitals were full. Many lost their lives. Cremation and burial grounds had queues.

Saurav tried to help the people of his city in whatever way he could. He tried to direct people to hospitals where beds were available, gave medicine and food to the needy, and arranged for plasma donors for patients who were in dire need.

Saurav did everything that he could to help people. He organized his party workers to help the citizens and made these attempts, both in his personal and professional capacity.

After a few months, Covid-19 cases decreased in his city. The public was full of praise for Saurav and his party. They acknowledged the manner in which Saurav had served the people selflessly, without caring for himself. Saurav was happy that his work had been recognized. He did not want anything for himself.

Then came the vaccines. Saurav was relieved that the world would get respite from this dreaded disease. The frontline workers, like the hospital staff and policemen, were the first to be vaccinated. Then came the turn of the elderly to be vaccinated. Saurav tried to lend a helping hand here too. He ensured that the people of his locality got the vaccine.

Then came the second wave of Covid-19. This wave was deadlier than the first. Many fell prey to the disease in Saurav's city and succumbed to it. Saurav had just taken one dose of the vaccine and was due for his next dose in a week's time.

But as usual, Saurav went about his work. This time, he was unlucky. He was struck with the disease. During the first few days, he was fine. He only had a mild fever and a cough. However, all of a sudden, his oxygen levels plummeted. Luckily, his workers rushed him to the hospital nearby, and he was given oxygen. For the next four days, he was on oxygen cylinders. His condition stabilized and slowly, he started recovering, although he still needed oxygen for a few hours.

The cases in the city increased and the hospital was full of patients. The doctors and nurses were busy and overworked. Saurav appreciated the effort that the hospital staff was putting in and was grateful to them for looking after him with such dedication and care.

A young woman named Mrs Nandi called Saurav on his cell phone one day, asking for help. Her husband, who was in his early thirties, was in a bad state due to the disease. He required oxygen and the hospitals were full. She had been turned down by every hospital. She had a six-month-old baby to take care of. She sounded desperate and almost became hysterical on the phone. Saurav heard her and asked her to come to the hospital where he was admitted.

Saurav made a decision. He called the doctor and asked to be discharged. The doctor was horrified upon hearing this.

'You are not out of the danger zone, Mr Sen,' said the doctor.

'It is okay. I would like to give my bed to the young Mr Nandi who requires it more than me,' said Saurav.

'But, Mr Sen—' started the doctor.

'Doctor, I have lived my life to the fullest. And anyway, I feel better now,' said Saurav firmly.

Although the hospital authorities and the doctors were reluctant to release Saurav Sen, they acquiesced to his demand after his persistent requests. Mr Nandi was admitted in his stead and was taken to the intensive care unit, where he struggled for his life.

Meanwhile, Saurav Sen returned home. But that very night, he developed breathing complications and passed away.

He had known that he would not survive if he returned home. Yet he gave up his life to save another person. Mr Nandi survived, but he could not thank his benefactor in person. Saurav Sen died the way he lived—selflessly.

The Prophecy

Mohan Sharma lived in a small town called Rangia. He was a young man of twenty-five. He lived with his parents and two siblings, a brother and a sister who were both younger than him. He was of average height, medium build, and a pleasant demeanour. He was employed in the local State Bank of India as a clerk.

Mohan had always been a disciplined person. In fact, his parents had no problems while bringing him up. He always listened to them, was a loving brother to his siblings and had a cordial relationship with his friends and neighbours. He did not get into arguments with anyone and he could always be relied on whenever there was a crisis. Many took advantage of him, but he did not seem to mind. He always liked to help others.

Since his childhood, Mohan had always been very religious. He would go to the temple every week and pray regularly. He would fast on certain days and strictly follow rituals on auspicious occasions. He believed in astrology. He would religiously show his horoscope to astrologers every year and would do whatever the astrologers thought would appease the stars.

Mohan also dressed according to the seasons. If the season was winter, he would wear his woollens, even if it was not cold. During the rainy season, he would be found carrying an umbrella. He was always prepared for all sorts of eventualities.

His seniors relied on him because he was so dependable and his juniors took advantage of his good nature. The customers at the bank would seek him out as they knew he would help them. He was always on time for work and was among the last to leave.

One day, he heard that a famous astrologer was visiting the nearby city of Guwahati. He wanted to travel to Guwahati and meet the astrologer. If all the advertisements on television were to be believed, the astrologer could correctly predict the future. In fact, a lot of politicians and well-known personalities were making a beeline to meet the astrologer.

Mohan, too, tried to make an appointment. He was overjoyed when he found out that he could meet the astrologer on the third day of his visit to Guwahati. He planned to take his horoscope along and decided to take a leave from the bank.

On the day of his appointment, he was up very early. He barely slept at night. He planned to ask the astrologer a few things about himself. That way, he could plan and prepare for his future. It was not that he had major problems, he just liked to be prepared.

Mohan reached the appointed place much before his allotted time. He waited patiently for his turn. There were many people waiting to see the astrologer. Finally, he was ushered in. The astrologer was a middle-aged man dressed in a saffron-coloured dhoti and kurta. He was bespectacled and had sandal paste smeared on his forehead. He looked at Mohan with a keen eye, observing everything and taking in the details. The room was dimly lit and many incense sticks had been burnt, giving the space a slightly smoky effect. The whole ambience overwhelmed Mohan.

The astrologer asked him to be seated and took down the details of his birth, like the date, timing, place, etc. Mohan was prepared with them all.

'So what is it that you want to know?' asked the astrologer. 'Have you come with any specific purpose?'

Mohan replied, 'I just want to know what the future holds for me.'

The astrologer nodded and started making calculations. Mohan waited patiently. After some time, the astrologer started frowning and seemed to be intently studying something. Finally, after a good fifteen minutes, he looked up gravely.

'Young man,' said the astrologer solemnly, 'I am afraid your future is not very bright.'

'What do you mean?' asked Mohan, deeply disturbed upon hearing his words.

'In fact, to put it bluntly, you don't have much time left in this universe,' stated the astrologer quietly. 'As per my calculations, you just have a year.'

Mohan was shocked by this disclosure. He was bereft of speech for a few minutes. His face paled in fear. He started trembling and his heartbeat increased abnormally.

Then he gathered his composure.

'Is there no remedy? Can anything be done?' he asked with quiet desperation.

'Nothing can be done, my son,' replied the astrologer. 'We are mere tools in the hands of the Almighty.'

Mohan paid the astrologer his dues and walked out of the hotel. He did not want to go back home. He felt as though everything around him had crashed. He had come to Guwahati with such high hopes in the morning, and within minutes, his future had shattered.

Mohan did not know how he reached the banks of the Brahmaputra River. He sat down on the shore and gazed at the mighty river with unseeing eyes. He thought and thought. There was nothing he could do. He thought about his family. He thought about his friends. He thought about the girl he fancied and had been meaning to propose to. He thought about his work. Everything seemed meaningless now.

No, he would not tell anyone about his predicament, he decided. He did not want to alarm his family and be a cause for their unhappiness. He would keep it to himself. There was nobody who could help him in this matter in any case, so why should he make others unhappy. He would keep this fact a secret.

He sat for a long time near the river bank. He did not feel hungry or thirsty. He was unaware of the passage of time. For him, the world had come to a standstill. He was in turmoil.

'Why me?' he thought in despair.

His life had been progressing so smoothly. He was happy and he had tried to make others happy. He had planned everything so meticulously. He was hardworking and sincere. Then why had god planned such a short life for him? All the hours that he had spent at the temple seemed meaningless now.

'God is unfair,' he thought. 'This should never have happened to me.'

Finally, he realized that it was getting late and if he did not make a move soon, he would miss the last bus home. He gathered his belongings and quickened his footsteps. He managed to catch the last bus and arrived home late. His mother was waiting for him anxiously and questioned him about the late hour. Mohan replied in monosyllables. On seeing his gloomy mood, his mother became silent. He did not feel like eating and he went to his room with the excuse that he had eaten and was tired. Sleep eluded him that night.

The next morning, as a consequence, Mohan woke up tired and irritated. He was late for work and though he tried to concentrate on his work, for the first time, he could not. His thoughts kept running off to the astrologer's prophecy. He felt listless and miserable. His co-workers were surprised because he had always been cheerful. Many of them asked him why he was morose, but Mohan just shook his head. He was left alone after a while.

Mohan was the first to leave the workplace that day. His colleagues thought that he was feeling unwell, and although they were surprised, they did not question him.

Mohan did not go home from work. He went to sit by the small river bank in his hometown. He did not feel like meeting anyone or talking to anyone. He was trying hard to come to terms with the prophecy. He brooded over his predicament and went home late that day.

Slowly, after that, Mohan changed. He was not aware of it. He became withdrawn and morose. He was always lost in thought. He slept badly at night and was late for work on most days. His work was affected and this was noticed by his colleagues and bosses. His friends tried to speak to him about the change they noticed, but he would not speak to anyone. His family was very worried by his behaviour, but the questions of his mother and siblings yielded no response. His friends, too, tried their best but Mohan remained tight-lipped and shrugged off their queries with a smile.

After a while, slowly, his family and friends left him alone. Even his colleagues decided that he should not be disturbed. This suited Mohan. He was now not answerable to anybody. He became even more immersed in his own problems.

The smiling, helpful man disappeared. In his place was a sullen and morose man.

Mohan lost weight as he had lost his appetite and sleep. He now had a dishevelled and unkempt look as he had grown a beard and had hollow, sleepless eyes. He was always late for work, and slowly, his boss stopped depending on him. Mohan was even warned that he would lose his job, but the warnings did not have any effect on him.

He stopped visiting temples and praying. What was the use of it? Nothing could be done.

But how long could he carry on in this manner? One thing led to another, and Mohan slowly took to drinking. This gave him some respite as he could forget everything temporarily while drinking. His family was now at their wits' end. His mother offered prayers in temples, trying to appease the gods and goddesses. She started visiting astrologers, godmen, godwomen, numerologists, psychics—anyone she believed who could help her son. But nothing helped. She even broached the subject of marriage with Mohan, thinking it might change her son, but he was disinterested. The rest of the family members dissuaded her from the idea and told her that another life would be spoilt if Mohan were to be married. His mother reluctantly withdrew her suggestion.

Months passed in this manner. His friends realized that Mohan was suffering from depression. They decided to take him to the doctor, but Mohan would hear none of it. He stopped talking to his friends. And this dissuaded his friends from pressuring him. If he did not want to be helped, how could they help him? He was slowly cutting off all the people who were close to him.

The situation at his workplace was also worsening. At first, his colleagues and bosses had sympathized with him, thinking that he was going through a bad phase. Slowly, due to his repeated errors, his share of work was given to others. His boss now depended on his juniors to deliver the work. And then, when he showed up drunk for work one day, his colleagues started to avoid him. His attendance in office became erratic.

His boss called him to his room and gave him a pep talk, but it hardly made any impact on him.

After a few months, he was issued a show-cause notice. This sobered him down a little. He decided to attend his office regularly, even if it was for a few hours, but he decided to keep to himself.

In this manner, a year passed by. Mohan was full of fear by now. His death might happen any time now. The only thing that he had forgotten to ask the astrologer about was how he would meet his end. Would he fall sick? Or would he fall prey to an accident? Or would somebody kill him? He was careful with his movements and did not have any enemies—but one never knew. So Mohan was extra cautious, expecting death at any moment.

Another six months passed.

By now, Mohan had stopped drinking every day. He could not think clearly if he drank too much. The last few months had required that he become cautious and he had lessened his alcohol intake.

Another couple of months went by. Now Mohan was puzzled. The astrologer had clearly predicted that he would live only for a year. But now it was almost two years since the prediction.

Could the astrologer have been wrong?

Mohan saw a small glimmer of hope.

But he was such a famous astrologer! Then again, he was also human and could err! Would he make such a big mistake? All these thoughts consumed Mohan day and night for a few weeks. Finally, he could bear it no more. His thoughts were driving him crazy.

He decided to go to his family astrologer and consult with him.

He did not tell the astrologer about his predicament, but he asked him to generally read his stars. The astrologer asked him for time and called Mohan the following week.

That week felt like years to Mohan. He was jittery and could hardly get any work done. On the appointed day, he went to the astrologer's house early, full of trepidation.

The astrologer smiled at him and said, 'You have a very good phase for the next few years.'

'Next few years,' repeated Mohan, disbelievingly.

'Yes, my boy,' replied the astrologer. 'Your stars are bright.'

'But, what about my life?' he questioned, bewildered.

'Life?' asked the astrologer, puzzled. 'You have a long one.'

'Are you sure?' asked Mohan hopefully.

'Of course I am,' snapped the astrologer, annoyed that Mohan was questioning his ability to read the horoscope.

Mohan was overjoyed. Suddenly the dark clouds seemed to have lifted from his life.

He hurriedly paid the token amount to the astrologer, touched his feet and bade farewell.

His joy knew no bounds. As he walked back to his village,

he thought long and hard. What a fool he had been. He had wasted two years of his life. And why? Just because of a prediction. He had lost friends and colleagues and distanced himself from his family. He had even lost the girl he loved because of his stupidity. He could have cross-checked and verified with other astrologers. He understood that he had believed the astrologer blindly and realized the folly of his superstitious ways.

Of course, this particular astrologer could also be wrong, he acknowledged, but should he live life according to predictions and superstitions? Realization dawned on him.

As he thought about the whole matter, he grew angry with the astrologer who had made the prediction about his early death. He had spoiled almost two years of his life because of a wrong prediction. He wanted to confront the astrologer. He had probably spoiled the lives of others with his wrong predictions as well. No, he could not let the astrologer go scot-free. He would make him answer for his wrong prediction that ruined his life, thought Mohan.

He reached home and searched for the contact number of the astrologer's assistant. He called up the assistant and demanded to speak to the astrologer. The reply from the other end stunned him.

The astrologer had expired shortly after returning home from Guwahati!

Mohan's anger cooled immediately. He was bewildered by the turn of events. He thought and thought and finally came to a decision.

No, decided Mohan. He would change for the better. He would give up his obsession with astrologers, superstitions and the like. He would make it up to his family, friends and colleagues. He would go back to his place of work and work hard with zeal and honesty. He would make up for all that he had lost.

He sent up a silent prayer to god. He needed to go back to Him. He would not fear what life had in store for him. He would live fully. He had learnt his lesson.

The Trip

Sanjiv was in his early forties. He worked in a multinational company. His wife, Janvi, was in her late thirties and was a homemaker. He had two sons, aged nine and seven, respectively. His aged parents lived with him in his four-bedroom apartment. His sister, separated from her husband, also lived with them.

Sanjiv's days usually started early as he had to commute to an office far from his home. When he came back from work, it was usually late. The house was entirely managed by his wife. She looked after his parents, the children and the house smoothly. She had a part-time maid who helped with the cleaning, but apart from that, she cooked the meals herself.

Since they depended on his singular income, Janvi decided to save every penny she could because theirs was a large family. She worked hard every day, without complain. This was her twelfth year of marriage.

She remembered the early years of her marriage. Life had been blissful then. Sanjiv was an attentive, loving husband, one that any girl would dream of. They lived in a small apartment. He was not bogged down with work and they went for movies and outings during the weekend. They visited friends and went out for coffee or dinner.

Janvi sighed. All these things seemed like a dream now. She could not remember the last time she had been out with Sanjiv. In fact, she could not remember the last time she had had a decent conversation with him.

After the birth of her two children, her father-in-law retired from service. Sanjiv worried about his parents and called them to stay with them. Her hands were full, looking after her two kids, in-laws and the household. Two years earlier, they had married off her sister-in-law to an affluent family. However, the young bride had trouble adjusting and within six months, she had separated from her husband and come back to live with them. Janvi's workload increased.

For the next six months, her sister-in-law, Sheila, wallowed in self-pity and refused to give her a helping hand. After that, she avoided helping altogether.

No wonder she could not adjust with her husband's family, thought Janvi uncharitably.

Sheila would not even make a cup of tea for herself or her parents. This irked her sister-in-law. When she tried to draw Sanjiv's attention to this, he would say indulgently, 'Let her be. She's been through a rough time.'

Sometimes, Janvi felt like an unpaid servant. She knew she could do nothing about it. Her husband was hardly home. He sometimes worked on weekends and also travelled on business trips. At times, she felt like she desperately needed a break for a few days. She wondered what would happen to the household if she fell sick. Who would do all the work?

Janvi, however, usually had a positive outlook on things. She tried to shrug off such negativity. However, of late, these thoughts had begun to haunt her frequently.

Sanjiv was too immersed in his work. Sometimes, she felt like he only came home to sleep and eat. If her in-laws had to be taken for a medical check-up, it was assumed that Janvi would do it. Parent-teacher meetings at the school were attended by Janvi. The society meetings at the housing complex were attended by Janvi. Be it weekly shopping, laundry or any other thing, all of it was attended to by Janvi.

Janvi had broached the topic of going on a short holiday. But Sanjiv's brusque reply—that the time was not right and who would look after his parents—silenced Janvi. Since she lived in the same city as her own parents, she met them once in a while, but she could not go and stay with them during school vacations as her other friends did.

Most of her friends were working, but they seemed to manage their work at the office and the home front easily. She yearned for some time with her husband, even if it was for an hour or two. That night, she broached the subject.

'Sanjiv, can't we go out for at least a dinner by ourselves?' she asked pleadingly.

'It doesn't look nice, Janvi,' replied Sanjiv, sighing. 'How do we leave the others out?'

'I could cook and keep everything ready,' replied Janvi with shining eyes.

'It's not about cooking, Janvi,' replied Sanjiv. 'Don't be selfish.'

Janvi was hurt. How had she been selfish? She spent every minute of the day running after the whims and fancies of her family. What about her sister-in-law? Sheila was always out with her friends for coffee or tea to the mall. If that was okay, then why was she being denied?

The next morning, Sanjiv informed her that he would be going to Chennai for five days for work. Janvi digested this piece of news. He was hardly home anyway. The children were having their annual exams and her evenings were spent teaching them their lessons. She would not miss him much.

Sanjiv came back the next week and attended office again. Meanwhile, the situation in the country was deteriorating. Many people who had travelled abroad had contracted the coronavirus and were suffering. The number of cases were beginning to grow as the virus was contagious.

The Prime Minister was a worried man. He announced the closure of educational institutions and imposed a travel ban outside the country.

Sensing that the situation might worsen, Janvi shopped extensively for her family. She replenished her groceries, which would last her at least a month. Her neighbours were doing the same things. She tried to procure all the essential items such as medicine, gas cylinders, etc. Her husband told her she was unnecessarily panicking, but she did not listen to him.

She had an uncanny feeling that the situation would deteriorate.

And sure enough, it did.

The Prime Minister announced a complete lockdown of the country on 24 March 2020. Movement was restricted, offices were closed, and travel was banned. Sanjiv was stunned. He could not believe it.

Janvi was happy that Sanjiv would be at home with her. Yes, she would have extra work, no doubt—her part-time maid would not be able to come—but she would manage, she thought.

After a long time, Sanjiv would be spending some time

with the family. But her husband seemed to be preoccupied. He was unhappy with the whole situation. She thought it had something to do with his work.

Janvi slogged day and night for two days. On the third day, their doorbell rang early in the morning. Curiously, she went to open the door. Who could it be amidst the lockdown? She found a couple of policemen in masks outside. They asked her whether this was Sanjiv Sinha's home? She replied in the affirmative. They stuck a notice on the wall which said the family had been quarantined.

'But why?' asked Janvi, astonished. 'My husband had only been to Bangalore.'

Meanwhile, Sanjiv had also come to the door after waking up.

'Madam, your husband had been to Bangkok last week,' replied the policeman. 'He was with a lady who has been hospitalized with Covid-19 last night.'

Stunned, Janvi turned to confront her husband. He did not deny, and evaded her eyes guiltily.

No wonder her husband had no time for her. He had cheated on her while she had been slogging for his entire family. And now he had put all their lives at risk! Covid-19 had exposed the sham that was her marriage!

The Winner

Meera was in her final year of college. She was an average student. She loved history and planned to graduate with history as her major subject. Her parents were school teachers. She was the eldest daughter and had two younger siblings, a brother and a sister. She was a pretty girl of good height and beautiful hair. She was shy by nature. Her pleasant disposition and amiable attitude attracted her friends. She was not very ambitious. She had a boyfriend named Mihir Baruah who belonged to an affluent family.

Meera had caught Mihir's roving eye when she was a fresher in college. He was a student leader and a member of the college's student union. He came to college on a flashy bike and was popular amongst the students. At first, Meera was astounded and embarrassed when she was singled out by Mihir. His friendly overtures overwhelmed her. She could not understand his interest in such a quiet and steady person as her, but slowly, she started enjoying the attention he bestowed upon her. She was envied by many college girls as Mihir was smart, good-looking and popular.

The first two years of college life passed by in a whirlwind of activities. There was college week, competitions, festivals and so many other memorable occasions. Life was fun. Meera and Mihir were together for almost all of the activities. Even the elections were fun. It was known to all in the college that the two of them were in a relationship with each other. Then, when Maya reached the final year, Mihir graduated and went to Guwahati University for further studies.

Meera was sad at first, but Mihir consoled her and said that it was just a matter of a year. She could join him at the university after her graduation. This cheered Meera. So she went about her final year, taking her academics seriously and preparing to go to the same university as her boyfriend.

Meera's final exams were approaching when she realized that she was pregnant. She went into shock. She could not believe it. She was horrified by the predicament. What was she to do now? She wanted to tell Mihir about her condition right away, but he was away at the university. She forced herself to calm down and think about it.

She decided to answer her papers and then break the news to Mihir when he returned from the university. She was sure that he would marry her after learning about her condition. It was very difficult for Maya to concentrate on her studies, but she willed herself to study. She finished her last paper and emerged out of the examination hall to find Mihir waiting for her. She was overjoyed to see him; he had surprised her. She could now tell him about her pregnancy instead of shouldering the burden alone.

Mihir took her to their favourite meeting spot—a secluded place by the Kolong River.

'I have something important to tell you,' announced Meera.

'What?' questioned Mihir.

'I am pregnant,' Meera stated bluntly.

'What!' exclaimed Mihir, his face turning ashen.

Meera was silent and she let her news sink in.

Mihir thought quickly.

'Abort it,' he stated.

'How can you say that?' Meera was shocked.

'Look, we are both studying. I am not earning. How can I support you and the baby?' reasoned Mihir. 'This is the best solution now,' he added persuasively.

'How can you even think of getting rid of the baby?' countered Meera accusingly.

There was a tense silence for a few minutes.

'No, I cannot do it,' Meera said decisively.

'Think rationally,' persuaded Mihir. 'I cannot support you or the baby. In fact, I will not even acknowledge the baby. It will never have my name. I have planned my future. I will be joining politics. I intend to be a people's representative. I cannot be tied down with an illicit child now.'

Meera looked at him with unshed tears in her eyes. She was in love with a person who had no scruples. What had she seen in him? He was shallow and only cared about himself. She knew that this was the end of their relationship. She walked away from him.

Meera was distraught. She had learnt about Mihir's real personality the hard way. He may be a leader, but she understood that he had no morals. He was not a strong person. She had misjudged him. How could she not see through him? She was heartbroken. Her dreams of a rosy future with Mihir had been shattered.

She walked home slowly, mulling over her next step. She

would have to tell her parents. She had no option. She was scared of their wrath.

She could not find the courage to tell them. She felt cornered, but she knew she could not delay it any longer. That evening, she broke the news to her parents. They looked at her in sheer disbelief and horror. How could she do this to them? Their reputation would be tarnished. They were respectable people. How would they face society?

They suggested an abortion, but Meera would hear none of it. Her conscience would not allow it. She had made a mistake, but she could not make a bigger mistake and feel guilty throughout her life. Over the next few days, the atmosphere in the house was tense. Meera was depressed. She did not know what to do. Finally, after four days, Meera was called by her parents. They gave her an ultimatum. She could abort the baby or leave home. Meera listened to them wide-eyed. She had not thought that her parents would abandon her. She was asked to give them her decision in the morning.

That night, Meera could not sleep. Tears flowed continuously from her beautiful eyes. She could not kill an innocent baby. She had nowhere to go, no one to turn to. What would she do? How would she survive? All these questions kept plaguing her throughout the night. She thought and thought but could come up with no solution.

At dawn, she came to a decision. She packed her clothes and certificates. She had a meagre amount of money that had been gifted to her. She told her parents that she would keep the baby, bid adieu to her siblings, and walked out of the house. She did not have any concrete plans, but she knew for sure that she would have to leave her hometown. Her parents were aghast by her decision. They had no option to offer other than an abortion. Society would shun them if their daughter gave birth to an illegitimate baby. They were helpless. She was a shame to them. They resolved that their eldest daughter would be dead to them.

Meera walked to the bus stand with her belongings. She thought that if she left town quietly, no one would know the reason for it. The reputation of her family would remain untainted, so the sooner she left town, the better for them.

However, she had not thought about her ex-boyfriend's plans. Mihir, like her family, did not want his reputation to be tarnished either. So he had spread a rumour around town that while he had been away, Meera had become pregnant with someone else's child. This rumour had spread through the town like wildfire. Meera could not prevent the news from spreading.

She met a couple of schoolmates on the way to the bus stop. They avoided her. She was puzzled. One woman from her locality stopped her and told her that she had brought shame to the locality. No one wanted to be associated with her. Meera realized that her secret was out. Everyone would now come to know of her pregnancy. This shook her to the core. She instantly realized that Mihir had leaked their secret. How could he have stooped so low?

Dejected, she caught a bus to Guwahati. Mihir was no longer her worry. What would she do? She had walked out of her home with false bravado. But where would she go? How would she fend for herself? Where would she live? Who would give her a job? She was not even a graduate!

After a couple of hours, she reached Guwahati. She was familiar with the place as she often came to the city with her mother to visit her aunt. Should she go to her aunt's house?

She could always try. At most, her aunt would refuse to keep her, but then she did not want to face the pain of rejection.

Meera decided to go to a small guest house near her aunt's house. She would spend the night there and look for a job after. She would have to find some way to earn money. Luckily for Meera, the guest house had a vacant room. She booked herself into a single room for the night. She had very little money with her. She would have to spend it carefully. Alone in her room, she contemplated her position. She would have to find a job which was not physically taxing. Otherwise, it would become difficult for her.

The next morning, she decided to look for jobs in the newspaper. She would go through the papers and then try her luck. No, she would begin by asking around in the guest house itself. She had no choice. She was desperate. She would do any sort of job. So she started by asking the receptionist if there were any jobs available. The receptionist replied in the negative. She started looking through the newspapers. She came across an advertisement in *The Assam Tribune*. There was a posting for the job of a teacher in a newly-opened residential school in Itanagar in the neighbouring state, Arunachal Pradesh. It was far from Guwahati, but that did not matter. She noted down the address and phone number. There were other job advertisements of sales representatives, receptionists, etc. She noted down the details and decided to try her luck.

She went to a phone booth and called the number of the residential school. A pleasant voice asked her for her particulars. Since she had not graduated, she was not very hopeful, but the person at the other end spoke to her for some time and asked her when she could come to visit for an interview. Meera was surprised and replied that she could come immediately. She knew that the meagre amount of money that she had would deplete even quicker if she were to travel, but she decided to try anyway. She tried not to think about what would happen if she did not get the job. The thought of being left with little money scared her.

In the evening, she headed for the bus station and boarded an overnight bus to her destination. She reached Itanagar in the morning. She found herself a room in a small hotel and rested for a while. Then, after bathing and changing into fresh clothes, she headed for the school. She met the principal and was interviewed. She realized that the post had not been filled up as there was a lack of teachers in the area. Since her graduation results were due, they checked her credentials and were satisfied. The job was offered to her.

Meera could not believe it. She had no experience in the field and had not even graduated. It had to be providence! The salary was not very high, but it would be sufficient for her.

'Beggars cannot be choosers anyway,' thought Meera. At least she would not starve.

The next important matter was finding suitable accommodation. She voiced her concern and was told that accommodation would not be a problem. Meera found herself renting out two rooms in a retired couple's home. They were warm and friendly towards her. Meera explained her financial situation to them and they were understanding. Meera was grateful that she had managed to find a job and a roof over her head in such a short time. She could not believe her luck.

And so, she settled into a routine. She started teaching at the school and adjusted to her new surroundings. She did not know anybody in the town and was thankful that no one knew about her past. Slowly, she was acquainted with her colleagues at the school and a few parents. In a couple of months, her pregnancy became apparent. But no one asked her any questions and she was thankful.

Meera's results were declared and she learnt that she had graduated. When she had ample time, she had wanted to do a Masters in history, but she didn't know if she could study after the arrival of the baby. She went for periodic check-ups to the local government hospital and had a smooth pregnancy.

Her baby, a daughter, was born in the month of December. It was a normal delivery in the local government hospital. School had just closed for winter vacations. Her baby had arrived at the right time. Meera was overcome with mixed emotions. She was thrilled to be able to hold her daughter, and at the same time, she was sad that the baby would not know a father's love. She vowed to do her best for her daughter. She would give her so much attention and love that her daughter would not feel the absence of her father or anyone.

Meera named her daughter Prisha, which meant 'god's gift'. After the arrival of her daughter, Meera's life changed. She had no time to brood or think about her misfortune. She had only one goal now: she would bring up her daughter to be a good human being, a strong and confident person with good values and morals.

Meera juggled her work and took care of her daughter with ease. The first couple of years were difficult for her, but as Prisha started attending school, life became smoother for Meera. Her salary was just enough for both of them. She continued living in the rented accommodation of the retired couple.

Sometimes, Meera felt very lonely. She yearned for her family and friends, but she knew that she was no longer welcome in her home or hometown. Her friends probably held good jobs, had gotten married and might be living happily by now. Whereas she was struggling as a single parent, trying to make ends meet. She could not blame anyone. She was solely responsible. Sometimes, she cursed her fate. She rued meeting Mihir. How different her life would have been if she had Mihir's love and support. But it was not to be. She had chosen the hard way. Her conscience had not let her kill her unborn child. Her daughter was god's gift. She would strive to give her the best.

Prisha was a happy, obedient child. She loved her school and was an understanding child. She helped her mother with her daily chores and did all sorts of odd jobs around her house. She was an average student and loved playing with her friends. When Prisha grew older, she began to question her mother about her father.

'Ma, where is my father?' Prisha asked curiously.

'You don't have a father,' replied her mother. 'I am your father as well as your mother.'

Prisha looked at her mother. The sad and determined expression on her mother's face deterred Prisha from asking any more questions.

Life carried on for Meera and Prisha. Prisha loved to race with her friends. When Prisha was twelve, she got noticed on the sports field. She was light and ran like the wind. She excelled at sports and sports day at school was the happiest day of the year for Prisha as she won a lot of medals and prizes. She would be the centre of attraction on sports day and she loved to see her mother smile with pride.

Some officials belonging to the Sports Authority of India were scouting for talent. They chanced upon Prisha. They were impressed by her ability to run. They approached Meera as they believed that with proper training, Prisha could be a good athlete.

Meera was taken aback. The officials told Meera that they believed Prisha had the potential to become a world-class athlete. They wanted to take her to Guwahati to train at the Sports Authority of India regional centre.

Meera was caught in a fix.

She did not know what to do. She had never lived apart from Prisha. How could her daughter manage without her? On the other hand, she knew that Prisha's life could change. She wanted her to excel in whatever she chose to do, but her daughter was so young. She had no one to advise her.

Meera was in a dilemma. She sought time. The officials assured her that Prisha's boarding, lodging and education would be taken care of. They told Meera that she could travel to Guwahati and have a look at the training centre.

That night, sleep eluded Meera. She looked at her daughter's young and innocent face. How could she send her away? She was only twelve. Her whole life revolved around her daughter. On the other hand, she knew she could not be selfish. If she refused, could she live with the guilt of not giving Prisha this opportunity? So many thoughts crossed her mind. Her lonely struggle. Everything she had done had been with Prisha in mind. Early in the morning, she made a decision. She would go to Guwahati and then make a final decision after seeing the environment.

Meera then fell into a deep slumber.

The next week, Meera and Prisha headed for Guwahati. She remembered the last time she had been to Guwahati. It had been over twelve years ago. She had been uncertain of her future and had come to the city without any plans. When she had left the city, she had not thought that she would come back after a decade. So much had changed. There were tall buildings everywhere. The streets had become wider. There was so much traffic. Meera felt lost.

They made their way to the training centre. Meera spoke to the concerned officials. She was taken around the complex and shown the facilities. Prisha was full of curiosity. She wanted to avail the opportunity as she loved sports, but at the same time, she did not like the idea of leaving her mother alone in Itanagar. The hostel was neat and clean. Meera spoke to the trainees individually to get a better perspective about the proposition. Finally, she was satisfied that the training centre would be good for Prisha.

She asked Prisha whether she wanted to train or go back with her. Prisha replied that she would love to train if her mother had no problems with it. Meera smiled at her daughter. It was time to leave Prisha.

And so began Prisha's training at the academy. Meera went back to Itanagar. She missed Prisha terribly and decided to bury herself in her work. She enrolled herself in post graduate classes to remain busy. During the holidays, she went to Guwahati to meet her daughter. Prisha came to Itanagar for a few days every year. They wrote letters to each other every week. Meera would write about every minute detail of her life and Prisha reciprocated by writing all about her life in the training academy.

Six years passed in this manner. Prisha turned eighteen. She was a hardworking child and had won many competitions at the national level. She had even been exposed to international level competitions as well.

Prisha qualified for the Olympics. Meera was ecstatic. Her coaches were hopeful. Since she was young, they opined that qualifying for the Olympics was a big achievement in itself for her and she would get the required exposure.

Prisha was thrilled at the prospect of representing her country. She knew that no one expected a lot from her. She could just watch the events live, but she vowed to herself that she would practice hard and give it her best. She knew that the country would be expecting medals from the boxers, wrestlers and shooters and there was no pressure on her.

On the day of the event, Meera woke early. She bathed and did her customary morning prayers and lit the lamp. She visited a nearby temple and paid obeisance to god. She prayed for her daughter's good performance. Then she went about her daily work calmly. She would not watch her daughter's performance on television. It would be nerve-wracking for her. Since it was a Sunday, there was no school.

Meera's phone rang at 10.30 a.m. It was the principal.

'Congratulations!' he shouted.

'For what,' queried Meera bewildered.

'Haven't you been watching television?' he asked. 'Prisha won the gold medal in the 100-metre race!'

Meera sat down in shock. Had she heard right? She was in a state of disbelief. She had never, not in her wildest dreams, thought that Prisha would be winning a medal in the Olympics, let alone a gold medal. She thanked god for her daughter's achievement. Tears streamed down her face. All her sacrifices had not been in vain.

After that, her colleagues and neighbours dropped in at her house. The small town rejoiced at the success of the young Prisha. Suddenly, Meera's house was full with people, some she knew, some she didn't know. Journalists thronged her house, from both print and electronic media. They wanted Prisha's mother's reaction. The television channels were live streaming. Someone had bought sweets and it was being distributed.

Prisha's classmates were rejoicing and doing a jig. Happy scenes streamed across television sets throughout the country. Prisha called her mother at the booth and could barely speak. It was an emotional moment for the mother and daughter. It was the happiest day of their lives.

Sleep eluded Meera again that night. She thought about how everyone had wanted her to abort the baby. She had taken a stand because her conscience would not allow her to abort an innocent baby. And although she had to undergo hardships and had been forsaken by her family and friends, Prisha's achievement had vindicated her decision. She felt at peace and was happy after a long, long time.

Prisha became a star immediately. She was the first female athlete to win a gold medal for the country. The President and the Prime Minister called Prisha to congratulate her. Prize money was offered by various states, athletic associations and sports bodies across the country. All kinds of gifts in cash and kind were offered to her.

Meera went to Guwahati to receive her daughter where Prisha was received by the Chief Minister himself. Mother and daughter hugged each other, happy tears streaming down their faces. There were huge crowds at the airport, people jostling to see the young and victorious athlete. The media had gone berserk. A state ceremony was hosted in Prisha's honour and she was offered the job of an officer in the home department by the state government in Assam. The government of Arunachal Pradesh and the Indian Railways also offered her high-paying jobs.

Prisha was spoiled for choices.

Prisha attended the state ceremony with her mother. At the ceremony, Prisha was felicitated by the Chief Minister, followed by the Sports Minister. All was fine till Meera realized who the Sports Minister was.

It was Mihir.

'He has achieved his dreams of becoming a politician,' thought Meera. When Prisha was asked to speak a few words, she stated that she was dedicating the medal to her mother, Meera. She asked her mother to come to the podium. As Meera walked to the stage, Mihir's face turned ashen. He looked at Prisha closely as realization dawned on him. There was no doubt in his mind. Prisha was his daughter.

As the programme came to an end, media personnel surrounded Prisha and asked her about her father.

Prisha pointed to her mother. 'She is both my father and mother. It is because of her sacrifices that I am here today,' she said.

Mihir stood rooted to the spot, thunderstruck. The girl who was now adored by the whole nation was his daughter, but he had forfeited the right to call her his daughter even before she had been born. He could never call her his daughter now.

He recalled how he had arrogantly asked Meera to abort the baby and threatened that she would never have his name. Now that right was Meera's alone. Prisha, 'the daughter of the nation', was solely Meera's daughter.

Trust

Ritu looked at the message on her cell phone and sat down on her bed. She was shocked. She read the messages again. She grew pale and trembled at the implication.

'It couldn't be!' she thought. 'Did he really mean it? What was she to do now?' Ritu was perspiring profusely.

Ritu was a nineteen-year-old girl based in Guwahati. She studied at Cotton College and lived with her mother in Panjabari. Her parents had divorced when she was just two years old. Her mother worked as a school teacher in a government school. The money she earned was not sufficient for them to survive, so her mother took tuitions to supplement her income.

Understanding the hardships that her mother had to go through, Ritu studied hard and helped her mother with the household chores. Ritu was an above-average student and after passing her twelfth standard examinations, she joined a graduation course with political science as her major subject.

She was a friendly girl and enjoyed going to college. She had studied in an all-girls school all her life and studying in a co-educational college was very new and exciting for her. She made a lot of friends in college.

She was introduced to Raj by one of her friends. Raj was her senior in college and also a rising actor. He was very popular and extremely good-looking. So when Raj singled her out and asked for her friendship, Ritu could not believe it. She had always admired him from a distance. He was always with a group of friends, having a good time. In fact, she wondered whether he even attended any of his classes. Girls vied for his attention and he knew his charms.

Ritu had caught Raj's attention because she was a pretty girl and very shy. Unlike the other girls, she did not 'chase' after him. This piqued his interest and he made enquiries about Ritu, attentive to all the information he gathered about her. She was interesting to him and completely unaware of her own appeal. Mutual friends introduced them as Raj had intended.

Ritu could not believe that Raj was interested in her. She was over the moon. He sought her out in college and took her for coffee in cafés and restaurants. He came to college on a bike and offered to drop her home. Ritu was, of course, careful to hide all these facts from her mother.

Soon, she began to bunk her classes and go out with Raj for movies and outings. Some of the girls in the college were envious of her good fortune. Ritu was blinded by all the attention that was being showered upon her. She was attracted to Raj and, very soon, she knew she was deeply in love with him.

Ritu mostly kept company with Raj and his friends during her college hours. When she was not with him, they were constantly texting each other, even late into the night. He constantly wanted to know her whereabouts, what she was doing, and Ritu was flattered by the constant attention. He asked for her photographs and she obliged. In return, she too asked for his photos.

Raj asked her to accompany him to the nearby hill station, Shillong. Ritu refused at first, stating that it was impossible for her to do so, but he kept requesting and begging her until she relented. She had one condition though: that they would only go for the day. Raj agreed.

Ritu lied to her mother and went with Raj to Shillong. The day was a romantic one and she enjoyed herself thoroughly.

This was just the beginning. They would steal away to nearby places for the day once or twice a month. On one such occasion, Raj booked a room in a picturesque resort. He had planned it well in advance. They became intimate after Raj kept persisting.

Then, Raj started demanding nude photos from Ritu. She was apprehensive at first, but she gave in to Raj's cajoling eventually. Raj even clicked nude photos of the two of them in compromising positions. Ritu did not object as she thought there was nothing wrong in giving in to his demands.

Several months passed when Ritu noticed that Raj was spending less time with her. His replies to her messages were less frequent. She was annoyed by his sudden lack of interest and she made her annoyance known to Raj, but he did not seem to be bothered. He did nothing to pacify her or rectify the situation.

Ritu soon noticed that he was beginning to spend more time with another group of girls. She was jealous as she watched the situation for a few days. One day, she could bear it no more and confronted him. Raj slapped her in front of everyone. She was shocked. She had never felt so humiliated in her life and so she decided to avoid him.

But Raj would have none of it. He asked her to accompany him to Shillong again. She refused, but this time Raj became violent with her. She was terrified. This was a totally different side to Raj and she had never seen him in such a mood before. She did not know what to make of it.

After two or three of such violent incidents, she decided to break off her relationship with Raj. She did not have the courage to tell him to his face and so she texted him her decision.

The reply shocked her. He had threatened her with dire consequences. He would post her nude photos on social media if she broke off her relationship with him.

What was she to do? He was blackmailing her. He would leak her photos and they would go viral and it would spoil her reputation. She was devastated. Had she been in love with such a vile person? She had been duped by his attractive personality. He had swept her off her feet and she had been blind to all his faults. She could not sleep that night.

The next morning, she decided to meet him in person. Raj had been expecting it. She pleaded her case and asked him for all her photos. He laughed at her.

'What do you want from me?' she asked in desperation.

'To continue our relationship like before,' he replied promptly.

Ritu felt defeated. The next couple of months were terrible for her. She could neither tell anyone about her problems, nor decide what to do. She could not eat or sleep properly and this tension was affecting her adversely. She would die of shame if her pictures were to be made public. Her life was a mess. Sometimes, in the dead of the night, she thought about ending her life, but then she thought about her mother. No. She could not bring such grief to her mother.

There had to be a way. Her honour was at stake. She was appalled by her naivety. Why had she gotten so carried away? She had not even thought about it and had agreed to all his propositions. Sometimes, she felt like she could do nothing to change the situation. He would always be able to make her do whatever he felt like doing. He wielded power over her with those revealing photographs.

Then one day, there was an awareness camp on narcotics and cybercrime by the Criminal Investigation Department of the state in their college. Ritu attended the camp and realized that there were many other victims like her. She had to file a complaint in the police station.

After a lot of thought, she decided to file a complaint. Mustering her courage, she went to the local police station. Luckily for her, the complaint was registered and assigned to a dynamic young police officer. He asked her not to worry.

Raj was arrested by the police. Ritu panicked because she had not expected such quick action to be taken. His friends at the college were surprised. They did not know what to make of it.

Raj had been so sure that Ritu would not complain about him and so he did not know why he had been arrested. When he was questioned, he decided to play innocent.

Then his house was searched and his laptop, pen drives and his mobile were seized. The police had arrested him based on a specific complaint. They searched his laptop and found out that there were photographs of several girls in the nude or in intimate positions. He was produced in court the next day and remanded in police custody for five days.

For Raj, those were the worst five days of his life. He had never been so afraid before. His family were shocked by the turn of events and were ashamed of him. They felt that he should be punished. He was then sent to jail after his police remand was over.

Ritu, on the other hand, was still afraid that Raj would harm her after he was released from jail. She attended college regularly, but she was always scared that Raj would appear, bully her and create a scene. Sometimes at night she would wake up in cold sweat.

After a month or so, on her way to college, she saw Raj. Her heart skipped a beat. What if he confronted her now? Raj had seen her, but he hurriedly turned away from her and changed his route.

Ritu was puzzled. Why had he done that?

Unknown to her, the young police officer had fixed her problem. Raj was made to strip at the police station and pose in the nude. His pictures were clicked in his birthday suit. He was threatened that if he bullied or blackmailed anyone in future, his nude photos would be plastered all over the town.

Value

'Time and tide wait for none.' That was so true, thought Mr Surjya Baruah. He was sitting in the balcony attached to his bedroom, soaking in the early morning sun. His blood report said he was deficient in Vitamin D. The doctors had given him medicine and advised him to sit in the sun and absorb its rays. He liked to sit outside his room early in the morning when there was peace and tranquillity in the house.

Mr Baruah was seventy-five years old. He had built the house twenty-five years ago. It was a huge house and he had built it with a lot of passion. The house had a huge garden in the front planted with hedges and a lot of flowers. There was a kitchen garden behind it and a small pond as well. The house itself had big rooms and all the modern amenities.

Mrs Baruah had objected to his plans. She had not wanted a huge house. She had wanted a house which would be easy to manage, with a small compound. But, as usual, Mr Baruah had overruled her objections and decided to go ahead with his plans. He had wanted his house to be grand and the cynosure of all eyes. He was so proud of himself.

He recalled his early years. Theirs had been an arranged marriage. He was in his late twenties and it had been five years since he had joined his father's business. He had picked up the threads of the business and had just started to expand. He had wanted to take his business to new heights, but his parents had wanted him to get married as he was their only son. His parents had arranged for him to be married to the daughter of their close friend. The bride-to-be was educated, homely and had a pleasant personality. Mr Baruah did not have any objection to the match.

After the wedding, Surjya went back to his work, devoting himself wholeheartedly to his projects. His wife, Rukmi, was a few years younger than him. Surjya had explained to her that he needed to focus on his business. She was understanding about his need to go back to work immediately.

Rukmi adjusted to her new home, learning the ways of her new family. As days passed, she slowly realized that to her husband, work would always remain a priority. She was disappointed that her husband spared very little time for her, but there was nothing that she could do about it. She was a gentle and meek person who did not really know how to stand up for herself; she felt intimidated by her aggressive husband, although he was always gentle with her.

Before a year of their marriage had passed, Rukmi was blessed with a son. Surjya was ecstatic. He adjusted his schedule to spend more time with the baby.

Rukmi gave birth to two more children over the next five years, another son and a daughter. She became busy with her children and her husband became busy with important projects, tours, and other important work.

Rukmi had her hands full with three growing children

and her ageing in-laws. Sometimes, she voiced her concerns to her husband regarding his long absences. Surjya gave her money and asked her to hire as much help as she required for the smooth functioning of the household. There were domestic workers to look after his parents, his children, his house and he also bought Rukmi a vehicle with a driver. He gave her enough money to splurge on herself as well. He never questioned her about how she spent the money. Whenever Rukmi desired his presence for important occasions like birthdays, anniversaries or parent-teacher meetings, he excused himself on the pretext of important work and tried to compensate for his absence with expensive gifts or money. He believed that money was the answer to all problems in life.

The children grew up without the presence of their father, even during important occasions. It was their mother who looked after them during their sicknesses; it was their mother who they turned to whenever they had problems; it was their mother whom they shared their secrets, fears and joy with. At times, they wondered why their father could not give them time, like other fathers. Rukmi however, would explain to them that their father was different and had important work to do. It hurt Rukmi to see the children grow up like this, but she vowed to be both a father and a mother to them. She tried to fill the void in their lives by being present for them.

Rukmi's in-laws were full of praise for her. To them, she was the daughter they never had. They could not understand where they had gone wrong in their upbringing with their son. He only understood the importance of money. They had educated him in one of the best boarding schools in the country, and then he had studied in colleges and universities abroad. He came home on vacations and holidays, but what his parents failed to realize was that their son did not understand the importance of family because he had never been a part of it.

He did not shrug off his responsibilities towards his family, but he did not participate in any activities with his family either. He did not realize how important family time was. He believed he had given his wife everything he could by giving her money. She had never lacked anything material. He prided himself on being a capable provider. He worked hard for his family and genuinely believed that he was doing the best he could for them.

A few years later, his parents passed away, one after the other. He had provided them with the best medical care that was available and was satisfied that he had done his best. He did not realize that even during their final moments, they had craved his company. Rukmi looked after them till the very end like a loving daughter.

Surjya then put the children into the best boarding schools available. Rukmi did not want to send her children away at such a young age, but her husband believed that it was in the best interest of the children. He convinced her that she was being selfish. Rukmi stood her ground as long as she could, but finally, when the children reached the sixth standard, all of them were sent to prestigious boarding schools in North India.

Surjya then made plans to build a huge house. Rukmi had wanted a small and manageable house, but Surjya would have none of it. He went ahead and built the house with the latest amenities available. His house was the talk of the town. Their friend circle envied the beautiful house with its well-kept garden.

Rukmi felt lost in the huge mansion. Her children were at boarding school most of the year and her husband was hardly at home. Her household help was efficient and did a good job of maintaining the house and gardens, but the large rooms felt empty, even though the rooms were decorated with valuable artefacts and paintings. The house did not feel like a home to her. There was no personal touch to the rooms. Everything was neat and had been kept precisely.

The house only filled up during the vacations. The children brought in warmth and laughter. Sometimes, they had their friends over for the day or for sleep-ins. Rukmi loved those times. She kept busy in the kitchen preparing their favourite dishes. The well-kept bedrooms were in a state of disarray during the time and there was loud music and noise. She looked forward to these wonderful times and dreaded the day when the children went back to the hostel. The house would become silent again.

Surjya and Rukmi entertained guests at times. These guests were usually people important to Surjya. They were powerful, important people. These lunches or dinner parties were formal affairs. Catering would be arranged from the best hotels in the city, even though Rukmi was a talented cook and had a good cook to help her. Rukmi never really felt involved in these parties. She didn't have to look after anything except dress appropriately and make small talk, but she knew it was important for her husband, so she never complained.

Rukmi had groups of friends over for lunch or tea parties sometimes. She was always there for her family members, especially when someone was in trouble. She was loved by her friends and family for her warmth and practical nature. She represented the family at all social events arranged by her friends and relatives. Surjya was never to be seen on such occasions.

A few years passed in this manner. The children had gone off to colleges abroad and they completed their education. Surjya had become a big businessman. He had two companies and wanted his sons to take over from him. His daughter was an artist and was not interested in his business. One by one, both his sons joined his companies and he slowly taught them the tricks of the trade.

His daughter got married to a friend's son and they moved to America. Then his elder son got married, but soon after Rukmi passed away suddenly. She had been feeling unwell for some time now. She had slowly brought it to Surjya's notice. He had asked her to consult the family doctor. The family doctor had advised her to go for a full health check-up. Surjya promised to take her for the check-up, but she passed away suddenly due to a stroke.

Surjya could not believe it. He felt lost. The children were grief-stricken. The eldest daughter-in-law took over the reins of the house and Surjya was relieved. He had someone to take over the burden of the house.

He worked for a few more years and then started having issues with his health. His sons suggested that he should retire. Surjya realized that this was a good suggestion. By now, his younger son had also married and he even had grandchildren. He could retire peacefully. His business was in able hands.

But before he retired, he had a stroke due to high blood pressure. His left side was left paralysed. He was hospitalized for the first few weeks and then brought home. His sons hired trained nurses to look after him. It took him nearly six months to recover. He had to undergo long sessions of physiotherapy. During this time, he missed Rukmi very much. She would have looked after him with love. But now, everything seemed mechanical. His daughter-in-law was out on most days, clubbing with her friends or out socializing. His sons dropped into his room once a day to enquire after his health. He wanted to discuss the business with them, but they would have none of it.

Surjya felt trapped. Trapped in his bungalow with no warmth. No one came to visit him. Not even his employees. His grandchildren were busy with their own routine. His sons were busy with work. His daughters-in-law were busy with their own lives. He was given food and medications on time. The only interaction he had was with his helps. His daughter paid him a short visit. He did not have any friends and no relatives came over.

He missed Rukmi with an intensity he had never felt before.

He did not understand that his sons did not have anything to talk to him about. The relationship between the father and the sons had always been formal. Rukmi had always been the provider. They were in awe of their father. He had not really been there as they were growing up, like other fathers. The children had envied other children, their contemporaries, and the easy relationship those children had with their fathers. For them, all their major decisions had been taken after consulting their mother. She had understood their emotions and had always been present for them. The children did not know how to relate to their father in the absence of their mother. They had always seen him as aloof, and even now, they thought he wanted to remain aloof.

Surjya realized that he had been wrong; in fact, he had been very wrong in thinking that money or material goods could buy happiness. He could not change himself at this age. He did not even know how to go about it. He only had himself to blame. However, he was not a person who would give up easily.

He decided to try.

The next day, when he was out in the veranda, he saw his eleven-year-old grandson in the garden with his mobile phone. He called out to him.

Riyan, his grandson, was surprised.

'Yes, Koka?' he asked.

'What are you doing?' asked Surjya.

'I was reading the news on my mobile,' answered Riyan.

'What news?' queried Surjya.

'It's about the family of a Covid patient,' replied Riyan. 'The patient expired at the hospital. The family could not perform last rites due to Covid protocols. But they asked the persons performing the last rites to hand over his valuables.'

Surjya was deeply disturbed by the news. Did his family not value the man? Would his plight also be like the dead Covid patient? He had never valued anyone else's feelings. It had always been his way or no way. If he died tomorrow, would his family miss him? Was he valued by his family?

Surjya was very disturbed. He prayed to god that he would not contract Covid and die because of it. He knew he had always disregarded his family, but when he died, he did not want his body to be cremated by strangers. He wanted to be mourned by his family in death. He wanted his family's love.

Vengeance

The college classes for the day had just ended. Rohan was walking out with his friends. It was not that he attended classes regularly, but today was an exception. Exams were approaching and he was low on attendance. As they filed out through the corridor, he spotted his sister, Ria, who was with her friends.

'Ria,' Rohan called out.

Ria turned to look at her brother and the girl next to her turned around as well. She was of the same height and build as Rohan's sister, but that was where the similarity ended. The girl had big eyes with long lashes, a sharp nose and a lovely complexion. She was breathtakingly beautiful. Rohan felt as though he could not breathe.

'Rohan?' asked Ria.

Rohan returned to his senses quickly. 'Tell Ma I will be late,' he mumbled quickly.

'Why?' asked Ria.

'I will be going to Raj's for his birthday party,' he replied.

'Okay', she said and continued to walk with her friends. Rohan stared at them both.

'Come on, Rohan,' said Raj. 'What's the matter with you?'
'I...who...?' Rohan muttered.
'Who is who?' asked Raj patiently.
'The girl with Ria?' questioned Rohan.
'Amrita,' replied Raj. 'Don't you know her?'
'I've seen her for the first time,' replied Rohan.

That evening, Rohan went home early from the birthday party. He did not enjoy the party. He needed to speak to his sister. He wanted to know more about Amrita.

Rohan's father was a politician and his mother was a high-profile lawyer. Both his parents were busy with their respective professions and had very little, rather no time for their children. To compensate for their lack of time, they spoiled both children with money. They lived in a sprawling mansion in an upscale part of the city. Materially, the children lacked nothing. They had both studied in boarding schools. After the completion of their twelfth boards, they had joined a prestigious college in their city. Being left alone in their childhood, the siblings developed a close bond.

Rohan reached home and started badgering Ria for information about Amrita. He was deeply attracted to Amrita and wanted to know everything about her. Ria was surprised by Rohan's questions. He had never shown an interest in any of her friends before. She teased him about it, but when she saw his serious face, she acquiesced.

Amrita was a brilliant girl. Both her parents were teachers in a government school. She was an only child and aspired to be a civil servant. She was a friendly girl and did not have a boyfriend.

Rohan was relieved to hear the last bit. He seemed to have fallen in love, something he had never believed in before.

He could hardly sleep that night. The next morning, he was up early and ready for college on time. This was surprising as Rohan always went to college late. He was rarely serious about attending college and he usually bunked the morning classes.

Ria raised her eyebrows when she came to the breakfast table and found Rohan eating.

'What is the matter?' she asked. 'How is it that you are ready for college so early today?'

Rohan just smiled.

'Okay, I get it,' replied Ria, coming to her own conclusions. 'I suppose the change has been brought about by your latest interest?'

Rohan just shrugged his shoulders.

The next few days, Rohan was regular at college. He attended classes and was on time for them. It was almost as if he had turned over a new leaf.

He tried to catch glimpses of Amrita. Sometimes, he saw her in the corridor, hurrying for her classes, and at other times, she was in the library or the canteen. He wanted to be introduced to her, but somehow the occasion for it had not materialized. He tried to find out all about her. He even followed her home from college one day. He made sure he was at a safe distance and that she did not know he was following her. He found her address and checked out her timings for tuition and her dance classes. He was obsessed with her and tried to learn every detail about her. At home, he badgered his sister for information. She would tease him mercilessly about his latest interest. Sometimes, his patience would wear thin when Ria refused to divulge information. Ria was fond of Amrita, but more often than not, she would end up giving Rohan the requisite information.

It was a Friday. The canteen was full, as usual. This time, Rohan was lucky. Amrita and Ria were together. Rohan felt a surge of excitement. On the pretext of speaking to his sister, he walked over to their table. Ria seized the opportunity and introduced her friend to her brother. Amrita was polite and friendly with him.

Rohan did not linger for long. He did not want to appear overeager. So he bade them farewell.

The chance meeting thrilled him.

Ria teased him at home, but Rohan did not mind. He was happy. He planned a strategy. The next few days, he pretended to accidentally meet Amrita in the library, at the market or on the streets. He would greet her in a friendly manner and Amrita reciprocated the greetings.

Slowly, as the accidental meetings became too frequent, Amrita became wary. Rohan did not have a good reputation in the college. His group of friends belonged to rich and powerful families. They took drugs and drank alcohol. They did not care about studies and attended college just to hang out with their friends. They were not serious about attaining degrees.

Amrita, on the other hand, had always been serious about her education. She was the topper in her class and she aimed to get through the civil services. She knew that her parents had a lot of expectations of her and she wanted to live up to them. So she worked even harder. She was friendly with everyone but did not want to have any romantic relationships with anyone.

She did not like the attention that she was getting from Rohan. She tried to avoid him. She tried to be formal and distant. Still, Rohan persisted, trying to strike up conversations, inviting her to the college canteen for tea or coffee, which she politely declined. She was friends with Ria and did not want to hurt her by speaking against her brother. She knew that the siblings had a very close bond and Ria could see no wrong when it came to her brother. Ria worshipped Rohan, so it was a difficult situation for Amrita.

One evening, while Amrita was walking home after finishing classes, she was waylaid by Rohan.

'Amrita, I want to speak to you alone,' said Rohan.

'What about?' questioned Amrita abruptly. She did not have a good feeling about this meeting at all.

'Can we go to a café nearby?' asked Rohan.

'I am in a hurry as I have tuition classes,' replied Amrita curtly.

Rohan had not prepared for this response.

'Actually, I love you,' he blurted out.

Amrita was stunned. She did not know what to say.

'I know this is sudden,' continued Rohan. 'But I would like your response.'

Amrita gathered her wits and immediately responded, 'Look Rohan. I do not have any time for romance right now. So my answer is no.' She ended the conversation bluntly. 'Please excuse me,' she said firmly and started walking towards her house, her cheeks red with embarrassment.

Rohan kept staring at her, not knowing what to do. His shoulders drooped and he went home feeling depressed. The next few days, he was very morose. He moped around the house. He did not attend college and lost his appetite. Ria noticed the change in her brother and cornered him. He confessed that he had proposed to Amrita, but had been rejected. Ria was angry with her friend, but she could do nothing.

After a week, Rohan was back in college. He had thought about his situation. He decided to pursue her relentlessly and convince Amrita. He was obsessed with her beauty and grace, and so he started stalking her.

Amrita grew frightened. She did not know what to do. She was wary of being alone. She decided that there was safety in numbers and she moved around with her friends in large groups. While going home from college, she ensured that she was with other friends or seniors. She made sure she was never alone. Rohan did not get a chance to speak to her as she was always in a large group.

A couple of months passed. Exams were approaching. Rohan could not concentrate on his studies. He wanted to make Amrita his at any cost. He could not bear the thought of Amrita sharing her affections with anyone else. She consumed his thoughts during the day and the night.

'No, Amrita is mine and mine alone,' thought Rohan. 'How can I ensure it?'

He pondered over it. He would try again. Perhaps she had changed her mind. Perhaps she wanted to be asked again. Why would she reject him? He had the looks, belonged to a rich and powerful family and he could give her anything that she desired. He knew her parents weren't very well off and it irked him that she should refuse his proposal.

He did not want to speak to her when she was with her friends and draw attention to himself. If she did not respond well, he would be very embarrassed.

One day, he found Amrita coming out of the library alone, heading to her classes nearby. He accosted her in the corridor and again pressed her for an answer to his proposal. He even asked her if she needed time. He was willing to wait, but Amrita replied in the negative.

This time, Rohan could not accept it. It was as though she had directly slapped him. His ego was hurt. Jealousy coursed through him when he saw her with other friends.

'No, her smiles had to be for me and only me,' he thought.

He thought and thought about his predicament. At last, an idea dawned on him. He carefully thought it through. He weighed the pros and cons. He would go ahead with his plans.

He could barely sleep that night and when he woke, he decided that he would put his plan into action immediately.

He rose early the next morning. He waited till the shops opened and made his purchase. He had had a long time to put his plan into action. He would bide his time. He patiently attended his classes. His mind was in turmoil, but nothing was visible on his face or in his demeanour.

When classes ended for the day, he took his bike and went ahead to a deserted stretch near Amrita's house. He had checked her out in the morning. She was wearing a black sweater over her uniform.

He did not have to wait long. He saw Amrita and her friend alight from a friend's vehicle ahead of him. They had gotten a lift from a friend. Usually, Amrita walked back with two of her friends who were her neighbours. But today, there was only one friend. He saw her from behind. He could recognize her anywhere even from a distance. The road was deserted.

He walked with long strides and when he had nearly reached them, he took out a small vial and uncorked it. He reached out and touched Amrita's shoulder. When she turned towards him at his touch, he threw the contents of the vial on her face.

There was a loud scream of pain.

Rohan stood rooted to the spot. The girl he had mistaken for Amrita was his own sister, Ria.

She was wearing Amrita's black sweater and was now screaming and writhing in pain. He had attacked her with sulphuric acid that he had purchased in the morning. Amrita looked in horror at the brother and sister as realization dawned on her that she had been the intended victim.

Ria lost one eye and was disfigured for life. She had to endure several surgeries and great pain. Rohan was sentenced to prison. His family was ashamed of his deed.

His punishment, however, was that he was responsible for causing immense pain and permanent disfigurement to the only person who worshipped him like a hero, his beloved sister, Ria.

War

Havaldar Jiten Saikia had joined the Indian Army in the year 1995. He was just twenty-years old when he joined the service. The army had conducted a recruitment rally in the small town of Dibrugarh. Jiten had just passed his twelfth grade examinations and many boys from his village had gone for the physical tests set by the army. He joined the boys of the village. The physical tests were tough, but as Jiten was physically fit, he cleared the tests without difficulty. He was one of the lucky few from his village to have made it; lucky as employment was hard to come by. His family was proud of him.

Jiten was the eldest son of Bireswar Saikia. His mother had passed away when he was seven years old. His father had remarried. Even though he could never forget his mother, he accepted his stepmother wholeheartedly. In the course of time, he had two stepbrothers. Bireswar showered his brothers with love and affection even though he was much older than them. The two brothers doted on him and the household was a happy one.

It was with a heavy heart that the family bade farewell to Jiten when he had to join the army. He had to undergo rigorous training after which he got his first posting in Jaipur.

Life in the army had its ups and downs. Jiten was a cheerful person and he made friends easily. His helpful nature endeared him to his colleagues. Every three years, his unit would change the posting of the recruits. So Jiten travelled to many parts of India over time. He saw the ways of life of other cultures and easily mingled with people from various states of India.

Jiten used to look forward to his yearly leave. He would come home on those occasions for a month or two every year and would spend time with his family. His brothers were growing up and would vie with each other for his attention. They loved listening to tales of his travels and work. He would bring his family small gifts and they would enjoy the surprises. His stepmother would make him dishes that he loved and it was always difficult for him to return to his posting, leaving his loved ones behind.

When he was twenty-five, Jiten's family decided that it was time he got married. They told him that they were searching for a nice girl for him. And so they decided on Tora, who lived in the next village. Tora's father was known to Bireswar and both families agreed to the marriage on the Assamese New Year in the month of April.

Jiten took a leave for a couple of months for his marriage. The wedding was a simple one, but there was great merriment. His brothers, who were now teenagers, enjoyed the family event and eagerly welcomed their sister-in-law to the family. This time, it was harder for Jiten to leave his family and his newly-wedded wife. Tora was tearful at his departure and her beautiful and sad face remained with him throughout his journey back to his unit.

The next five years were eventful for Jiten. His wife gave birth to two children. He could not be present with her during their birth, but he ensured that he was home during the first month of each of their lives. His responsibilities had increased. Earlier, he used to send money regularly to his father. But after the birth of his children, he created a bank account for Tora and sent her money every month.

Tora missed her husband's presence on important occasions, but she was a sensible girl and understood the difficulties of being an army man's wife. She was a practical person and wrote letters to her husband every week, apprising him of every incident in the household and the village.

Jiten's stepbrothers, Nagen and Romen, had now grown up. They were not particularly good at studies, and after failing their board exams, they decided to drop out. This upset Jiten because he had wanted them to graduate and be employed in good jobs. Unemployment was a big problem and their father was growing old. Jiten sent money regularly to his father, but he had thought that his brothers would get employed and this would provide their father with some economic relief.

His brothers were not trained for any other job and so, the two brothers decided to take up farming. Bireswar owned ten bighas of land, which was used for the cultivation of paddy. The brothers took to the fields and also started rearing cows and goats.

Jiten's posting kept changing at regular intervals. Both his children were growing up and attending school. Expenses were also shooting up. Jiten was promoted to the rank of a havildar. He continued sending money to his father and his wife and his brothers worked hard in the fields.

Then, Jiten's father fell sick and had to undergo an

operation. Jiten was worried and came home to look after his father. His father expressed his wish to see both Nagen and Romen married. Both of them got married in due course. Jiten was instrumental in helping them financially with the expenses for their marriages. He knew his responsibilities.

After a few years, Bireswar passed away one winter. He was suffering from various ailments and had been bedridden for some time now. Jiten reached his village in time to perform the last rites and realized that his responsibilities had now increased.

Jiten started sending money to his stepmother now. His brothers had come of age, and their families had also grown now. Jiten had built two more rooms in the old house so that his wife and children could live comfortably. But tragedy struck once again when his stepmother passed away suddenly after a couple of years.

This time, Jiten could not attend the funeral. His unit had been posted in Kashmir. The situation between India and Pakistan was deteriorating every day. Small skirmishes were taking place at the border. The army kept thinking that very soon there would be a war. Jiten's unit was posted in one of the forward bases. They were on alert, but the morale of the unit was high.

Jiten was due for a leave, but he knew that under the circumstances, leave would be difficult to obtain and it would be a long time before he could go home. Tora knew that her husband had been posted near the border and she kept track of the news anxiously and prayed for the well-being of her husband. Like all army wives, she dreaded war and the horrors that it entailed.

Although times had changed and they had cell phones

now, Tora continued her practice of writing long letters every week. However, the advent of war made her write to her husband more frequently.

It was in such a situation that Jiten received Tora's letter. It was a long letter and he sat down to read it. The contents of the letter shook him to the core.

Jiten's stepmother had left a will behind. She had divided the agricultural land between her two sons, Nagen and Romen, equally. The old house was left to the two brothers jointly.

Jiten was left with only the two rooms that he had built.

Jiten was shocked. He re-read the letter a couple of times. He could not believe his predicament. His stepmother, whom he had respected and loved, had ousted him from the family land. Tora wrote that Nagen and Romen had connived together and gotten the will signed by his stepmother. Jiten felt sick to the core.

Meanwhile, there was an alert. The enemy had started an attack. Jiten's unit got ready to fight. Jiten ran and equipped himself, despite his turmoil. Years of discipline and training had taught him to be prepared for any eventuality. This was his chance to fight for his motherland. Although he had served in the army for twenty-five years now, he had always been posted at peaceful places.

He was calm. He was not afraid of the outcome. He would go out and do his best. If need be, he would offer his love for his motherland. It was better to fight a known enemy than an enemy within. In this instance, he at least knew who his foes were. The unknown enemies within his family and friends were much more dangerous.

He was ready to fight.

Acknowledgements

Reading fiction has been a favourite pastime for me. I love reading short stories and novels. So much so that I have been dreaming of publishing my works of fiction from a young age. I continued reading, but could not spare time to write. Many busy years passed by while I played the roles of student, wife, mother, police officer and so on. Deep within, the desire to write burned strong. I realized that I had to fulfill my dream.

I am thankful to my soulmate Partha for encouraging me in this endeavour. He read the first draft of each story diligently, giving his honest opinion. On days when I tended to procrastinate, he would motivate me. But for him the book would never have seen the light of day.

My children Arshia and Chandril have been supportive, providing me with the 'necessary space' to write peacefully and indulge in my favourite pastime.

I thank my siblings Nandini, Sandeep and Krishnadeep for always being there.

I thank my sister-in-law Upasana Mahanta, and, Samrat Sinha for the interesting conversations and ideas which resulted in a couple of stories.

I thank Jaideep Mazumdar for reading my stories and giving me feedback.

I would like to express my gratitude to all my English teachers for instilling in me the love for English literature and language.

I also thank the editorial team of Rupa Publications for guiding me with their valuable suggestions. I would like to thank Amrita Chakravorty for the beautiful cover. And a special thanks to Dibakar Ghosh for all his help.

I must mention my friend Nikita Barooah, with whom I can have heart-to-heart talks at any time of the day, and night.

I thank Sankarjyoti Nath for helping me out with the technical issues. He has been immensely supportive and patient, assisting me whenever I needed help.

This book would not have been possible without the good wishes of my family, friends and support staff.

The
Homecoming
and Other Stories

Indrani Baruah was born and brought up in the small oil town of Digboi in Assam. After finishing her schooling from Carmel Digboi, she went on to top her batch in English Literature from Dibrugarh University. She has completed her Masters from Gauhati University and is currently an Indian Police Service officer posted in Assam. She is married to her batchmate in service, Pulhatarathi Mahanta, and is a mother of two lovely children and a golden Labrador. Her interests include reading, gardening and designing.

She can be reached at indranipmahanta@gmail.com

8